P9-CME-653

★ THE ★
Aurora County
ALL-STARS

Other Books by Deborah Wiles

Each Little Bird That Sings

One Wide Sky: A Bedtime Lullaby

Love, Ruby Lavender

Freedom Summer

★ THE ★
Aurora County
ALL-STARS

Deborah Wiles

HARCOURT, INC.
ORLANDO AUSTIN NEW YORK
SAN DIEGO TORONTO LONDON

www.HarcourtBooks.com

Portions previously published as the short story "Moves the Symphony True" by Deborah Wiles, *Boston Globe,* 2005

Library of Congress Cataloging-in-Publication Data
Wiles, Deborah.
The Aurora County All-Stars/Deborah Wiles.
p. cm.
Summary: For most boys in a small Mississippi town, the biggest concern one hot summer is whether their annual July 4th baseball game will be cancelled due to their county's anniversary pageant, but after the death of the old man to whom twelve-year-old star pitcher House Jackson has been secretly reading for a year, House uncovers secrets about the man and the history of baseball in Aurora County that could fix everything.
[1. Baseball—Fiction. 2. Death—Fiction. 3. Pageants—Fiction. 4. Sexism—Fiction. 5. Race relations—Fiction. 6. Mississippi—Fiction.] I. Title.
PZ7.W6474Aur 2007
[Fic]—dc22 2006102551
ISBN 978-0-15-206068-8

Map by Finesse Schotz and House Jackson
Compass holder, Melba Jane Latham

Text set in Dante
Designed by Lydia D'moch

First edition
A C E G H F D B

Printed in the United States of America

For Steven Malk,
shortstop

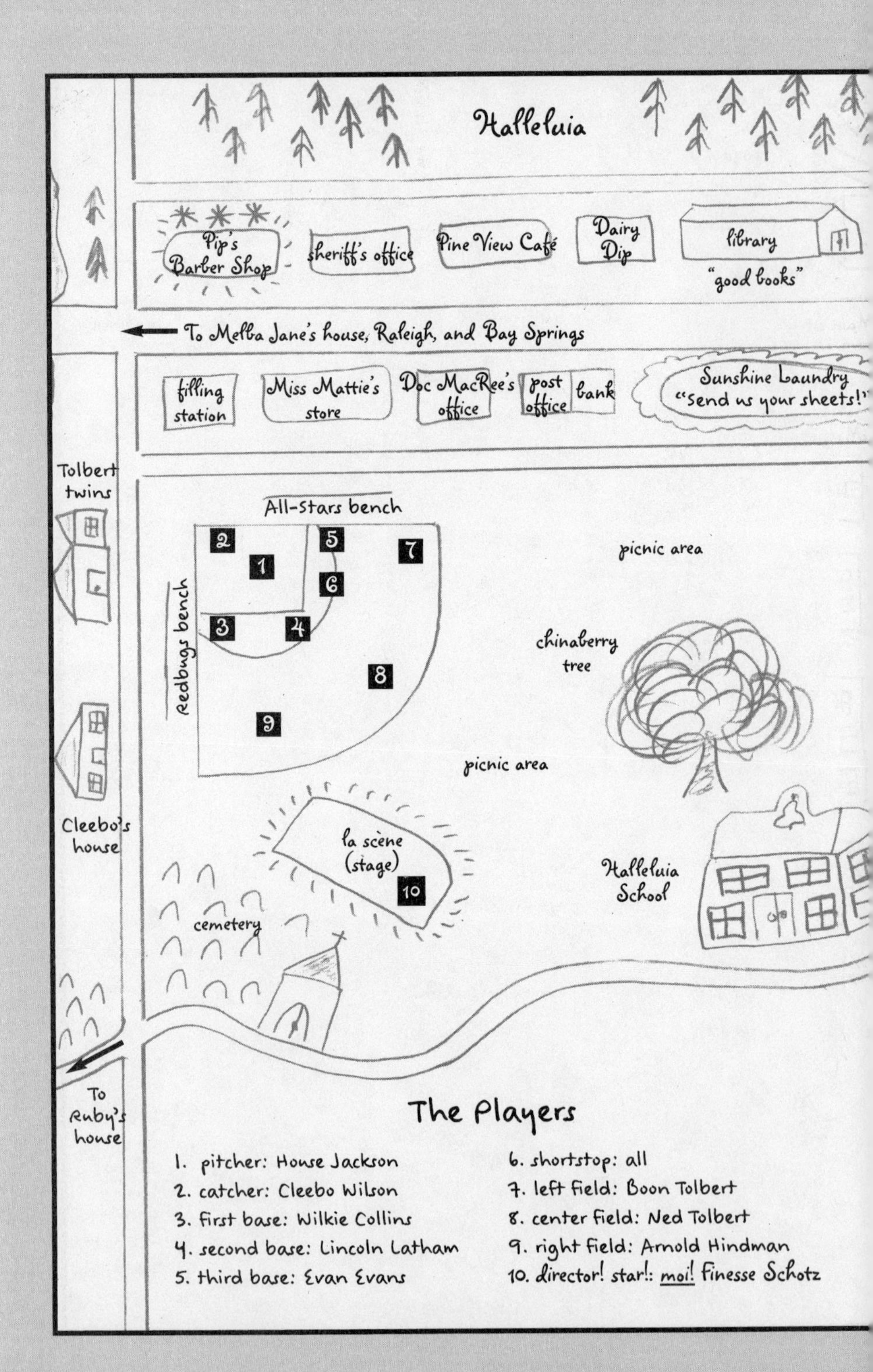
Halleluia
Pip's Barber Shop
sheriff's office
Pine View Café
Dairy Dip
library
"good books"
To Melba Jane's house, Raleigh, and Bay Springs
filling station
Miss Mattie's store
Doc MacRee's office
post office
bank
Sunshine Laundry "send us your sheets!"
Tolbert twins
All-Stars bench
redbugs bench
2
1
5
6
7
3
4
8
9
picnic area
chinaberry tree
picnic area
Cleebo's house
la scène (stage)
10
Halleluia School
cemetery
To Ruby's house
The Players
1. pitcher: House Jackson
2. catcher: Cleebo Wilson
3. first base: Wilkie Collins
4. second base: Lincoln Latham
5. third base: Evan Evans
6. shortstop: all
7. left field: Boon Tolbert
8. center field: Ned Tolbert
9. right field: Arnold Hindman
10. director! star!: moi! Finesse Schotz

Doc MacRee's
pond
To
Snapfinger
Mabel
Middle School
Pip's garden
Pip's house
Main Street
To Jackson and the prestigious Lanyard School
Miss
Mattie's
cotton
pond
barn
piney
woods
corn
kudzu
gate
To town
honeysuckle
bush
Mabel
Mr. Norwood's house
woods
path
To town
House's
house
Jackson's
Mowing
and
Small Engine
Repair
pecan trees

Courtesy of the Charles E. Feinberg Collection, the Library of Congress

This is what you shall do: Love the earth and sun and the animals, despise riches, give alms to every one that asks, stand up for the stupid and crazy, devote your income and labor to others, hate tyrants, argue not concerning God, have patience and indulgence toward the people, take off your hat to nothing known or unknown or to any man or number of men, go freely with powerful uneducated persons and with the young and with the mothers of families, read these leaves in the open air every season of every year of your life, re-examine all you have been told at school or church or in any book, dismiss whatever insults your own soul.

—*Walt Whitman, from the preface to the first edition of* Leaves of Grass, *1855*

People ask me what I do in winter when there's
no baseball. I'll tell you what I do. I stare
out the window and wait for spring.

—Rogers Hornsby,
second baseman, St. Louis Cardinals

Baseball Rules and Bylaws for the Aurora County All-Stars

By House Jackson, captain and pitcher, and Cleebo Wilson, catcher, and the rest of the team, signed below

We agree:

Seeing as how the nearest official Little League teams are in Rankin and Jones counties, we hereby declare ourselves our own team, the Aurora County All-Stars. Here are our rules.

1. NO GIRLS.
2. We play every day. We play in the rain. We play if it's cold. We play if it's hot. We play until dark or until too many kids are called home. Then we play catch.
3. If less than nine kids show up, we play flies and grounders. If more than nine kids show up, we make two teams.
4. Three strikes make an out and three outs make an inning. No exceptions.
5. No spitballs. Spitting is allowed.

We share balls, bats, gloves, and gum (not chewed).

6. If a batter hits the chinaberry tree or the schoolhouse, it's an automatic home run. No one has ever hit the chinaberry tree or the schoolhouse.
7. Balls hit into the cemetery stay there.
8. Every July 4 we play a real game with the Raleigh Redbugs. It's our one big game of the year and we promise never to miss it.

Signed in blood (not really) by the aforementioned and also by:

Wilkie Collins, first base
Boon Tolbert, left field
Ned Tolbert, center field
Lincoln Latham, second base
Arnold Hindman, right field
Evan Evans, third base

Please do not remove this notice
from the telephone pole by the backstop.

To me, every hour of the day and night
is an unspeakably perfect miracle.
—Walt Whitman

Mr. Norwood Rhinehart Beauregard Boyd, age eighty-eight, philanthropist, philosopher, and maker of mystery, died on a June morning in Mabel, Mississippi, at home in his bed.

He died at the simmering time just before daybreak. Crickets tucked themselves under rocks for the day. Blue jays chitter-chattered in the pines. High above the tree-tops, cirrus clouds wisped across a slate blue sky.

Mr. Norwood Rhinehart Beauregard Boyd lay un-breathing on a feather mattress surrounded by a carved rosewood bed frame with a high headboard that he had bought in Madagascar on his travels many years ago, be-fore he closed himself up in his house with his treasures.

All night long the June bugs had *tap-tap-tap*ped against the glass panes at the open bedroom window, trying to buzz into Mr. Norwood Boyd's room and touch the lamp-light. As the light came into the day, the hard-shelled little insects fell into an opening between the glass and the screen, where they hummed together at the bottom of the window in soft confusion. Outside the window, deep in the tall weeds, a garter snake slithered in search of mice. It was June 17. A Thursday.

Mr. Norwood Boyd died a quiet death attended by sky, clouds, crickets, birds, bugs, snakes, and one human being: House Jackson.

House Jackson, age twelve, crackerjack baseball pitcher, obedient son, and keeper of his own counsel, had arrived just before the simmering time. He eased himself gingerly into a ladder-back chair next to the carved bed. He held his breath as he watched Mr. Norwood Boyd breathe and stare at the ceiling in a faraway silence. Instinctively—for it had been his habit—he reached for the book on the bedside table. *Treasure Island*. He opened it to the page that had been saved with a ribboned bookmark, and read out loud in a mechanical voice: *Still, Silver was unconquered. I could hear his teeth rattle in his head; but he had not yet surrendered.*

At that moment, Mr. Norwood Boyd surrendered. He closed his eyes and opened his mouth. A rattling sound came from his throat. The smell of Mr. Norwood's rattled breath made House blink and sit back in his folding chair. That breath—the sound of it and the smell of it—traveled the entire room, spangling the air like a salute, as if that breath was a last farewell to the big old bed, a last farewell to the lighted lamp, a last farewell to the rose-patterned carpet, to the bureau where the clothes were kept, to the bedside table where water shimmered in the glass, and to House, who had been faithful.

When there was no more rattle and no more breath, House did as he had been instructed to do. He called Doc MacRee's office from the big black telephone beside Mr. Norwood Boyd's bed. His fingers trembled as he dialed, and his voice cracked as he tried to speak.

"Mr. Norwood Boyd." He was out of breath.

"Who is this?" asked a cranky-voiced Miss Betty Ramsey at the doctor's answering service.

"He's . . . dead." House felt the truth tingle across his shoulders, up his neck, through his scalp. He reached under his baseball cap and gave his head a small scratch.

"Is this a joke?" Miss Betty did not like jokes.

"No, ma'am," House whispered. His pale cheeks were on fire—he could practically hear his freckles sizzle.

Miss Betty's voice was high and nasal: "Is that you, Cleebo Wilson? You scoundrel! I'm calling your mama right now—she will whip you good! This is not funny!" House couldn't think of one useful thing to say. Miss Betty waited. "Hello?"

House put the telephone receiver back in its cradle as quietly as he could, as if he were handling a sleeping baby. Miss Betty's voice squeaked, *Who's there? Who's*—and then it was gone.

House licked his lips and stared at Mr. Norwood Boyd. He had half a mind to touch him, but he didn't. His mother had died at home six years ago, and he had wanted to touch her, too, but he hadn't. He thought about that moment now, of how he had somehow known that the body lying on the bed was no longer his mother. She was no longer there. And now Mr. Norwood Boyd was no longer here.

House glanced out the window where the sun was beginning to light up the day. It would be a hot one. Soon the whole town would know about Mr. Norwood Boyd's death. Kids would talk and the stories about Norwood Boyd would surface. The old rumors would rise and kids would have a heyday.

And there was nothing House could do about that. What could he say that would change anything? No one would believe him, anyway, and he'd never hear the end of it. It was best to keep his secret and to tell none of them.

He rubbed his open palms across his face and stood up. It had been a hard morning—an unbelievable morning. And today there would be more hard things. As soon as the sun blazed high in the morning sky he was going to have to face an enemy. A girl.

Swallow your toads early in the day, his mother used to say, *and get the hardest things over with first.* When he was six, his toads were easy to understand: *Make your bed! Clean your room! Vegetables!* As he got older, toads got harder to swallow: *Apologize! Be responsible! Tell the truth!* Now that he was twelve, his toads were life-sized and impossible to face, much less swallow—but he would do it.

He stared at a cobweb in the corner of the room. He had already faced death; he could face his toad this morning.

House took a last look at Mr. Norwood Boyd. He would go home now. He would take his sister, Honey, to pageant tryouts because he said he would. Then he would go to baseball practice. He would pitch like Sandy Koufax, his favorite baseball player of all time on his favorite team of all time, the long-ago Los Angeles Dodgers dream team of 1965. Koufax had pitched a perfect game in 1965, even when his arm felt like it was about to come off. House knew about pain like that.

Yes, that's what he would do. He would face his toad and he would get his life back to normal with the baseball team, the game, the summer. And no one would know that he had sat in Mr. Norwood Boyd's ghostly home this morning, watching a dead man decompose.

★ 2 ★

A man has to have goals—for a day, for a lifetime—and that was mine, to have people say, "There goes Ted Williams, the greatest hitter who ever lived."

—TED WILLIAMS, LEFT FIELDER, BOSTON RED SOX

The sound of fat tires crunching over the pea gravel at the front gates to Mr. Norwood Boyd's driveway shocked House out of his reverie. He almost bit his tongue as he leaped to his feet. Outside, car doors opened. Shut.

"How are we going to get in there?" Sheriff Taylor's voice sifted through the windowpanes.

House scooted out of Norwood Boyd's bedroom at the front of the house, sprinted down the wide hallway filled with photographs, dodged around the chairs in the dusty dining room, and jumped off the back-kitchen door stoop. He slid along the side of the house, his heart banging against his ribs. Kudzu vines slithered away from the driveway gates like snakes, as they were hacked and pulled down from the other side. Any minute now that gate would swing open. House parted the thick, leafy branches of a giant honeysuckle bush beside the front porch and crawled into what he knew was a good hiding place. It was cool and cavelike inside the honeysuckle bush. There was plenty of room. And House was not alone.

An old pug-dog with bulging eyes shivered herself sick inside the branchy cave. She stared at House with a pitiful look. "Hey, Eudora," House whispered. "Hey, girl." He scratched her between her ears. Eudora closed her eyes and gave a tiny sigh.

"What am I going to do with you?" said House. "I got baseball practice this afternoon." He would pitch and his best friend, Cleebo Wilson, would catch. Together they would work on House's fastball, now that his elbow seemed to be back in business. It had taken the better part of a year to get the elbow in good shape. The whole team was counting on that fastball to help them beat the Raleigh Redbugs in the big game on July 4. They had just over two weeks to be ready to pull off a victory.

House scratched Eudora under her collar—it made a crinkling sound. "You got something stuck in here, girl?"

The big gate in front of Mr. Norwood Boyd's creaked open at the same time that House pulled a piece of paper from Eudora's collar. It was rolled like a scroll, and his name was written on the outside of it—HOUSE—in an old, careful script. House stared at it. He felt the sweat stand out on his face. He had seen that handwriting before.

The gate clanged back against the iron fence and a cushion of kudzu. House shoved the note deep into his pocket and watched through the leafy branches of the honeysuckle bush, his heart pounding in his chest, as Bunch Snowberger and Sheriff Taylor entered and then left the house with Mr. Norwood Boyd between them on a stretcher, covered with a white sheet from head to toe.

"I'll call the county and get someone to board up the place tomorrow, before the curious arrive," said Sheriff Taylor. "Somebody's bound to get hurt out here—this place is falling apart."

The stretcher was swallowed up into the hearse. The double doors closed behind it like a tomb. Mr. Norwood Boyd was carried away, and House was left alone with a frightened, lonely dog and a note burning a hole in his pocket, just waiting to be read.

Cicadas called from the trees. Frogs sang from the pond in the back pasture. The sky was now a brilliant, empty, bright-morning blue.

The dog grunted. House rubbed her back and smelled her old-dog smell. "It's over, Eudora," he whispered.

But it was not over. It was just beginning.

Mr. Norwood Rhinehart Beauregard Boyd left behind a collection of black-and-white photographs, a library filled with musty books, and an ancient, pug-nosed, white dog named Eudora Welty. Later, when the long mystery that was Norwood Boyd unraveled and summer revealed its secrets, some folks would say it was the note that changed House's life forever. Others would say it was the dog. But it was neither the note nor the dog.

It was the pageant.

Morning Edition, June 17

The Aurora County News

Happenings in Halleluia

By Phoebe "Scoop" Tolbert

Heart palpitations and two days at the hospital notwithstanding, here I am, a little late with the news but with a lot of catch-up!

In a landslide vote at Miss Mattie Perkins's mercantile last week, the town council voted to give the director's chair for the Aurora County Birthday Pageant to Miss Frances Schotz, age 14, local theater talent and former Miss Sparkle Pants of Aurora County.

Frances moved with her family to Jackson last year, where she attended the Lanyard School for her eighth-grade year, concentrating on dance and foreign languages. She brings to the pageant director's chair extensive theater experience at Mabel Middle School, her alma mater, where she began her career as a tomato in a production of "The Long Hot Summertime." She is a natural choice to direct a pageant that will be performed entirely by children. She will live with her great-grandfather in Mabel this summer in order to be available to us and our pageant.

All children ages 14 and under are welcome to audition for the pageant. The most exciting news is that the pageant will be funded (indeed, was proposed) by Our County's Own Dr. Dan Deavers of the television soap opera "Each Life Daily Turns" (which can now be viewed on a gigantic television at the Sunshine Laundry in Halleluia every weekday at noon—"Watch While You Wait!"—but this is a topic for another article). Dr. Dan will leave his longtime home in Los Angeles for an overdue vacation—he will come home to attend the pageant! He will no doubt survey our young ones with an eye toward future stardom for a few.

Mamas! Sign up your children for Hollywood!

I have learned that to be with
those I like is enough.
—WALT WHITMAN

House and Eudora Welty came through the piney woods together. Eudora stumbled over tree roots and slipped over the pine straw that layered the woods path from Mr. Norwood Boyd's home to House's. It was a short trip, but Eudora, who was old and round, had to stop and rest every few minutes. "Good girl," said House every time Eudora rose to her stubby feet again. They walked out of the woods and onto a rutted dirt lane that hugged the pines and led to the house.

Honey Jackson, age six, aspiring dancer and lover-of-life extraordinaire, sat barefoot and cross-legged at the top of the front-porch steps. She wore her best pink leotard and tutu. Around her neck, hanging from some string, was a pair of toilet-paper-roll binoculars. Behind her, in a short, straight row, sat seven small stuffed animals—her audience.

"House!" she shouted, scrambling to her feet. "House, where *have* you been! I've been waiting for you all the live-long day! Daddy! House is here!"

Honey twinkled down the steps and raced across the dirt yard for House, who was nearing the pecan trees in the front yard. Then Eudora Welty rose from her resting place next to a thicket of blackberry vines, and Honey's world changed. She stumbled to a stop, whipped her binoculars to her eyes, and squealed. Eudora Welty plopped into the dust with a frightened thud.

"You brought me a *dog*!" Honey whooped. "Daddy! House brought me a *dog*!"

"What?" Leonard Jackson pushed open the screen door and appeared on the front porch, his face dotted with left-over shaving cream.

"Look, Daddy! A *dog*!" Honey ran right past House without so much as a never-you-mind.

House watched as Honey instinctively stopped short of the trembling Eudora Welty. She tiptoed toward her with her arms out as if she was a ballerina swan approaching her hesitant partner. Then she squatted so low in front of Eudora that her bottom swiped the dirt. She put her smooth, young face directly in front of Eudora's wrinkled and snuffling one. They blinked at each other.

"How are you, son?" asked House's father. He wiped his face with the towel on his shoulder.

"Fine," said House. He reached the porch, adjusted his baseball cap, and peered up at his father.

His father gestured toward Eudora Welty. "I see where you came from," he said quietly. "Did you spend the night there?"

House shook his head. "Eudora came and got me." He shoved his hands into his pockets and discovered his note there again, like a surprise. He had read it now a dozen times on his short walk through the woods. "She scratched on the screen door by my bed. I can't figure out how she knew where to find me."

"How about that?" said his father. He stepped over Honey's stuffed animals and sagged himself down onto the front-porch steps. "Is it over, then?"

"Yessir." House licked his lips.

Leonard Jackson bunched the towel in his rough hands. Three of his fingers wore Band-Aids. "Did you call Doc MacRee?"

"Yessir."

"Good. Did the undertaker come out?"

"Yessir. I hid in the bushes and watched."

"Why did you hide?"

House shrugged. "Didn't want to talk to anybody."

"I see." Leonard Jackson reached out and gave the brim of House's baseball cap a tiny tug. "How are you, son?"

The tender way he said it made the back of House's throat ache, the way it did when he was about to cry. He blinked back tears and blurted, "I don't remember what time I'm supposed to take Honey to the audition." It occurred to him that suddenly his mind was shot through with enormous blanks.

"You don't have to go," said his father. "I'll call Mose and tell him I'll be over later. I can take Honey."

House shook his head. "No! I mean...no. I'll go—I want to go."

"You do?"

House fidgeted. "Not really."

"What, then?"

House reached for the sunglasses that perched on the porch railing. He shoved them onto his face with both hands. "I got a toad to swallow."

His father's face slowly widened into a smile. "Your mama." He gave his head a small back-and-forth, remembering. House teared up at the words.

"Have some breakfast first, then." His father stood and flipped his towel onto his shoulder. "About Mr. Norwood. I'm proud of you, son. I know it was a hardship."

House shrugged. His head ached from weariness.

"Want to tell me how it was this morning?"

"Maybe later," said House. He was leaking all over the place. He slipped two fingers under his sunglasses and wiped his eyes. "Let's eat."

"Later then," said his father. He disappeared into the house. House put his sunglasses on top of the bucket of baseballs by the door. He cast a look in Eudora's direction.

Honey now straddled Eudora Welty. She had her arms under the dog's belly and was trying to raise her to her feet.

"I need help!" she shouted.

"She can do it herself, Honey," said House. "Give her some room."

Honey stepped over the dog and trotted to the porch. She turned and slapped at her thighs. "C'mon, doggie!"

Eudora wagged her curlicue tail.

House whistled. "Eudora!"

Eudora struggled to her feet, shook herself, and began a wobbly walk up the curved lane to the porch.

"YouDoggie!" said Honey. "That's such a good name, House!"

"Eudora," repeated House.

Honey sighed with happiness. "YouDoggie, I love you!" She hugged her brother. "Wherever did you find her, House?"

House told Honey that he'd found the dog whining in a thicket, which was true. He didn't tell her about the note, which felt like the size of a brick in his pocket. He knew what he had to do. When everyone went to bed he'd go back to Mr. Norwood Boyd's house by himself.

"Hoooooouse!" A coffee-colored boy on a licorice black bike careened around the curved lane and into the front yard, driving recklessly, making a beeline for Eudora Welty.

"Hey!" House jumped and waved his arms over his head.

"Cleebo!" screamed Honey. "Stop!" She lunged for Eudora and covered her with her tutued body. "YouDoggie!" she sobbed as she waited for the end to come.

You gotta be a man to play baseball for a living, but you gotta have a lot of little boy in you, too.
—Roy Campanella, catcher, Brooklyn Dodgers

Cleebo dragged a leg in the dirt and turned his bike so sharply it nearly fell on him as it scattered pebbles and pecans and raised a rooster tail of red dust.

"Hey!" He hopped on one leg while bobbling his bike and himself upright. His catcher's mitt waved back and forth on the handlebars.

"Cleebo!" House tried to pick up Honey but she was stuck to Eudora like a fly to a swatter. "You're going to kill somebody like that someday, Cleebo."

"Not today!" grinned Cleebo. He stared at Honey and the white lump cowering under her.

"What's that?"

Honey detached herself from Eudora and dusted herself off.

"It's YouDoggie!" She puffed with pride. Her binoculars were crushed. "She's my *dog*!"

"That's a dog?" Cleebo cocked a jet-black eyebrow in Eudora's direction.

Honey patted on Eudora, who had seen more excitement in one morning than she'd seen in a lifetime.

"When did y'all get a dog?" asked Cleebo. He wore blue jeans with neatly ironed-in creases down the front of each leg. Even his T-shirt was crisply creased.

"Just now!" Honey held her head high.

"Where'd you get it?"

"House got her!"

"Yeah? From where?"

"Breakfast!" Leonard Jackson called from the kitchen.

Cleebo leaned his bike against a pecan tree. "Can I eat with y'all?"

"You always eat with us," said House.

"Watch out for my audience!" Honey left Eudora Welty long enough to put her audience back in the basket they lived in when they weren't watching her dance. She spoke their names as she put them tidily away: "Liesl, Friedrich, Marta, Louisa, Kurt, Gretl, Brigitta!"

Cleebo readjusted his baseball cap. "I don't get it."

"And I'm Maria!" said Honey to her basket of children.

"I was a nun, but now I'm in love with Captain von Trapp and I'm going to be your dancing and singing mother!"

"You're not supposed to get it." House took the basket for his sister. "C'mon, Maria, let's eat."

Honey pressed her face to the screen door. "Daddy! Can YouDoggie come inside?"

"Are you sure that's a dog?" asked Cleebo, as the three—four—of them went in to breakfast.

Eudora Welty ate three platefuls of scrambled eggs and drank an entire bowl full of water. Honey watched in fascination.

"Come eat, Honey," said her father.

Honey hung her smashed binoculars on the back of her chair and plopped herself down at the table. "I have come to a big decision, Daddy."

"Do tell."

"I am going to leave my audience at home for the tryouts. I'm going to take YouDoggie instead!" House and his father exchanged a look. Honey forked a bite of scrambled eggs into her mouth and talked around it. "And... I am going to tap-dance!"

"You don't have tap shoes," said House. He used his fork to push his eggs around on his plate.

"Can we get some, Daddy?" asked Honey.

"I don't see why we gotta go to this stupid audition," said Cleebo. He poured himself a glass of orange juice. "I ain't gonna be in any pageant. We got our onliest ball game that day and I told Mama I wasn't—"

"You gotta be in the pageant!" interrupted Honey. "It's for all the kids!"

"I'm not a kid," said Cleebo.

Honey blinked. "What are you?"

"I'm a baseball player." Cleebo drained his orange juice. He wiped his mouth with the back of his hand. "I'm gonna play in the All-Star game on July Fourth. Forget that pageant."

"Your mama said she signed you up," said Honey in her most grown-up voice. "We saw her yesterday at the Piggly Wiggly—she was buying a whole grocery buggy full of starch for the Sunshine Laundry! She said your clothes are going to be the crispiest in Aurora County!"

Cleebo groaned. House stuck him in the ribs with the tines of his fork and mimicked the new radio ad:

"Sunshine Laundry!
Send us your sheets!
Under new management!
We can't be beat!"

Cleebo shoved House until his chair almost tipped over. "Cut it out, House!"

Leonard Jackson sat back in his chair with his coffee cup. "You're not eating, House."

"You *gotta* be in the pageant," cried Honey, trying to be heard. "All the Mamas were talkin' about it yesterday, right, Daddy?"

"Right," said her father. He put his cup down and wiped his mouth with a napkin.

Honey hopped off her chair. "Frances Schotz is the director!"

Cleebo snorted. "Watch your elbows, House!"

House shoved Cleebo. "Watch your crispy T-shirt!"

"Time to go, boys." House's father stood up and gathered plates.

"House started it," said Cleebo.

"Shut up, Cleebo." House clenched and unclenched his left fist. Sandy Koufax had crushed an artery in his left palm in 1962 and had developed gangrene in one of his fingers, but he still pitched.

"Don't say shut up," said Honey in a solemn voice. She patted Eudora Welty. "You didn't hear that, YouDoggie."

Leonard Jackson clattered plates into the sink. "I've got Mose Allison's yard to mow and a delivery to make but I'll be home after lunch. Come on, I'll give you a ride."

Cleebo tugged on his baseball cap and entreated House as they walked outside. "I checked with the rest of the guys—everybody's signed up for this stupid pageant, thanks to their mamas—everybody but you. You're team captain—what are we gonna do, House?"

"I don't know," said House.

"Well, you gotta know soon. The guys are countin' on you . . ."

"I'll think of something." He had no idea. Facing a toad was one thing. Swallowing it was another.

House and his father stood on the porch together, as still as two tree trunks, while Cleebo retrieved his catcher's mitt from his bike handlebars and Honey coaxed Eudora to the truck.

"Call me if you need me," said Leonard Jackson.

"Yessir," said House.

"Have you seen Frances since she's been back?"

"Nossir. Not yet." House stuck his sunglasses in his back pocket and felt the bend of his elbow as he did so.

"Maybe she's less hazardous after a year away," said his father.

"Maybe," said House. His mind ticked around the word *hazardous.* Hazardous was going to Mr. Norwood Boyd's empty house alone in the middle of the night. The place was full of shadows and felt haunted, even in the middle of the afternoon.

He grabbed his glove from the porch swing and a baseball from the bucket next to the door. "Heads up, Cleeb!"

Cleebo whirled. "A backdoor breaking ball and he's got it!" he gloated. "You oughta play me at first base."

House shook his arm. The elbow felt just fine. In 1965

Sandy Koufax had pitched the World Series for the Dodgers even though his elbow had turned black with pain. "Nobody else can catch like you can," House said. "Let's go."

The sign on the side of Leonard Jackson's truck read JACKSON'S MOWING AND SMALL ENGINE REPAIR. In the back of the truck sat two lawn mowers, a red wagon with a toaster in it, and an oscillating fan for the Sunshine Laundry.

The road was dusty and hot. They passed cotton growing in fields that stretched to the horizon. Houses dotted the roadside along with patches of gardens. An old tree sported a tire swing hanging from the sturdiest branch.

Soon they passed the house of Mr. Norwood Rhinehart Beauregard Boyd. A mountain of kudzu vines was strewn alongside the closed driveway gates.

"Hey! Lookee there!" Cleebo nearly gave himself whiplash.

House had to look. His heartbeat thrummed in his ears.

"What's going on?" Cleebo craned his neck out the window.

"I think they're getting ready to sell that old place," said Leonard Jackson.

"Sell it!" said Cleebo. "What about Baby-Eater Boyd?"

"Excuse me?" said House's father.

Cleebo stole a glance at Honey, who was absorbed in

looking out the opposite window with Eudora Welty and describing to her every detail of the passing landscape. Cleebo brought his voice down to a hush. "Everybody knows there's the ghost of a million babies in that house!"

House stared straight ahead and tried to breathe normally. Cleebo poked him in the side and hissed. "What about Baby-Eater Boyd?"

Twilight Edition, June 17

THE AURORA COUNTY NEWS

MURMURS FROM MABEL

By Phoebe "Scoop" Tolbert

One simply cannot buy carrots at the Piggly Wiggly in Mabel, Mississippi, without running into The Mamas. The Mamas congregate wherever Jell-O is sold, laundry is washed, and potluck is served. They generate a never-ending stream of talk and swapped recipes wherever they meet, which is almost everywhere, almost all day long.

The Mamas and their grocery buggies formed a *fort* in the produce section of the Piggly Wiggly this morning, making my grab at the cantaloupe impossible. The good news is that one can catch up on the most interesting conversation just by being near The Mamas and leaning over the cucumbers.

Which is where I observed Leonard Jackson (buying apples to make his late wife's famous applesauce cake for the Methodist church bake sale) and Gladys Knight Schotz (in town to deposit her daughter,

Frances, with her great-grandfather for the summer) in deep conversation about the Aurora County Birthday Pageant. It is shaping up to be a dramatic few weeks in Aurora County!

It seems that Leonard's son, House, has not forgiven Gladys's daughter, Frances, the faux pas she committed last summer when, in the middle of Schotz's Barber Shop, in the midst of a vigorous interpretive dance to commemorate the Summer Solstice, Frances collided with House as he was exiting the barber chair, thereby causing a colossal crash whereby hair and beauty accoutrements went flying from here to Kingdom Come along with House and Frances. House's left elbow was broken in two places. His pitching elbow. There went the one and only game the Aurora County boys play each year, against the Raleigh Redbugs. There went several family picnics in the weedy ball lot behind Halleluia School at 4pm sharp on July 4. (I should know: My grandsons, the Tolbert twins, play in the outfield and I always bring the deviled eggs in a Styrofoam cooler for a protein pick-me-up during the seventh-inning stretch.)

For her part, Frances suffered fractures of three fingernails and a bruised clavicle, not to mention humiliation galore... although there are those who say that, when it comes to Frances Schotz, humiliation is a relative term.

Be curious, not judgmental.
—Walt Whitman

"Darlings! *Mes amours! Biquettes!*" Frances Schotz, age fourteen, skinny and bumpy as a green bean, hair twisted into a wiry black propeller on top of her head, was in her glory. She sashayed into the small crowd of kids sitting in the shade under the chinaberry tree behind Halleluia School and flashed a smile so bright it prompted House to put on his sunglasses. "Welcome, everyone!" she warbled. *"Bienvenue, tout le monde!"*

House felt the hairs on the back of his neck stand at attention. There she was: his toad.

"What's she sayin'?" asked Cleebo. He and the rest of the Aurora County All-Stars sat at the back of the crowd and stared at Frances as if she'd just stepped out of a UFO.

"I think she's speaking Egyptian!" said Boon Tolbert.

Ned Tolbert, center fielder, shook his head in exasperation. "I told my mama I wasn't getting within ten feet of Frances after what she did to House last year, and she still signed me and Boon up for this thing."

"Mine, too," said Evan Evans. He squinted at Frances. "What's wrong with her?"

House poked his sunglasses farther up on his nose. "Same thing that's always been wrong with her."

"Nah, it's worse," said Cleebo. "She can't talk and she looks like a gooney bird!"

Frances's black hair was tinged with blue tips that matched her lipstick and fingernails. She wore black capris that stretched around her almost-curves and a silver shirt with colored sequins that caught the sun and shimmered against her caramel-colored skin.

"When can we leave?" Cleebo asked.

"Not now!" House cradled his left elbow in his gloved right hand and made himself stare at the patches of grass growing here and there.... At least it was cooler under the chinaberry tree.

"Not now?" Cleebo shoved his catcher's mitt into his armpit and gestured to his ball-playing friends. "Our mamas told us to show up and we did. Now we can leave, right?"

Boys murmured their agreement. "We got a game to get ready for," said Boon.

"I'm speakin' for all of us," said Cleebo. "When can we leave?"

House peered around the edge of the little crowd and saw Honey sitting cross-legged up front, mesmerized.

"When it's over," he said. Ballplayers groaned. *It's over.* A shudder skittered across House's shoulders. Mr. Norwood Boyd's whole life was over. His body was right now lying on a metal table at Snowberger's Funeral Home.

"Come to order, *mes amis*!" Frances tapped her clipboard with a pen. "I need your attention! *Faites attention!*" She wore high-heeled rhinestone sandals on her narrow brown feet and a million tinkly bracelets on each arm.

"You are the *chosen* ones!" she intoned. "My *bijoux*!" The chosen ones stared. Frances dropped her straw tote bag and flung her arms out for effect. "*Bijoux!* That's French for jewels!"

House pushed his sunglasses up farther on his nose and wondered what the French word was for toad.

Nervous laughter sifted through the crowd. "That's right!" said Frances. She motioned *Come on!* with her hands. "Laugh! Cry! Carry on! *C'est la vie!* It's what we're *here* for!"

"Not me!" piped Honey. She sat inches from Frances's painted toenails. She wore her pink tutu and had one arm wrapped around Eudora Welty. Eudora wore a tutu, too, also pink, around her neck. She panted nervously. Honey craned her neck up to Frances as she stated her purpose: "I'm here for the tryouts!"

Frances clasped her hands to her chest and made a face that said her heart was aching with happiness. *"Mais oui!* Of course you are!" With the tips of her fingers she slid her glasses onto her face—they'd been dangling around her neck on a jeweled chain. They were black, shaped like sideways teardrops. She gazed through the lenses, wide-eyed, at the assemblage.

She leaned toward them. They leaned back.

"Everyone gets a part," Frances declared in a confidential tone. "Everybody! That's *tout le monde* in French!"

Tout le monde began talking, all at once.

"Of course we all get a part," said Ruby Lavender, sitting plop in the middle of the crowd. "We're signed up against our will!"

"Well, I'm not!" said Melba Jane Latham. "Some of us *want* to help out our hometown!"

Ruby unwrapped a piece of Dubble Bubble. "I'm happy to help out," she said. "I just don't want to be in some stupid county anniversary pageant. We should just stick with the operetta in August like we always do." She shoved the bubble gum into her mouth.

"We've got a 200th anniversary and that's even better," said Melba Jane. She gazed at Frances, transfixed. "And this year, we've got professional help!"

Ruby hooted. Melba ignored her.

Frances clapped her hands together in tiny motions. Her wispy-thin bracelets tinkled against one another, like little bells calling everyone to order.

"Mes amis!" she said. "Silence, please! *Si-lence!* Time to get started! Remember, *everyone* gets a part!" She spoke in crescendo tones. "This is *our pageant* celebrating *our town*!" Her face took on an angelic look as she crooned in a come-to-glory voice, "It's positively Thornton Wilder!"

There was a smattering of applause. Kids looked around to see if there was anybody named Thornton Wilder among them, and Frances made a tiny curtsy.

"She's the picture of poise!" Melba whispered to Ruby.

"Who *is* she?" whispered Melba's little sister Violet.

Ruby popped her gum. "She used to be Frances Schotz." The bubble collapsed onto Ruby's nose. "She went off to boarding school last year, took too much French and drama, and turned into Marie Antoinette. Where's the guillotine?"

"I think she's amazing," sighed Melba.

"You would," said Ruby. She rubbed pink off her nose.

Frances pulled some papers out of her tote bag and clipped them to a clipboard. "I'll assign parts as they speak to me..."

"I don't want a part!" cried Honey. "I want to be a dancer!" She scrambled to her feet. Her legs, pale and thin as potato sticks, poked out from under her tutu. "House!"

Frances shaded her eyes with a jeweled hand and peered into the crowd. "House? House Jackson!" She blew a lofty kiss in House's direction. Baseball caps bobbed as boys in the back of the crowd laughed and slapped at House with their gloves. House tugged his baseball cap lower onto his head.

"Are we still friends, House?" Frances touched the tip of her tongue to her top lip as she searched the crowd. House hunched his shoulders up to his ears and studied his shoes.

Frances sighed and straightened her shoulders. "How about the rest of you, my former classmates? Are you still *mes amis,* even though I've been *absent* for a whole year?"

"We ain't *messy mees*!" cried Cleebo, poking his head up above the sea of caps. "But you sure are a mess!"

"Yeah!" said Ned Tolbert.

"Yeah!" cried Lincoln Latham.

Frances sniffed a short, dignified sniff.

"House?" Honey took a step away from Frances. She turned toward the small crowd. "House?"

Without a moment's hesitation, House popped up and made his way to Honey, his mind sputtering like a sprinkler. He'd had a matter of hours to get used to the fact that he'd seen a dead body, had made a phone call to report the death, and had adopted a dead man's dog. And now he had to deal with Frances Schotz, his toad, the former theatric terror of Mabel Middle School and the girl who had almost killed him last year.

He reached for his sister. "You can dance, Honey." He pulled his sunglasses down his nose a notch and forced himself to look Frances in the eye. "Right?"

Frances winked at House and struck a pointing-statue pose. "*Mais oui!* But of course! We need *les danseurs* for the *danse moderne*!" Then she offered a confidential look to House, leaned toward him, and whispered, "How's your elbow, darling?"

"It's fine," House said, in a voice as flat as paint. But that would not be enough to swallow his toad. Right now, it was stuck in his craw. He picked up Honey and held her in front of him for a moment, as if he might use her as a shield. Honey threw her arms around her brother's neck and pulled him close. House's sunglasses popped off his face and pancaked in the dirt.

"Good!" chirped Frances. She turned her attentions to the crowd. "*Tout le monde!* It has been so long since we've seen one another—allow me to reintroduce myself, *mes amis*!" She shone her radiant white-toothed smile on the crowd. "I have change-ed my name, *tout le monde*! I have a *nom de plume*! Please—*s'il vous plaît*! Call me Finesse!"

Murmurs of uncertainty rolled from kid to kid.

"She has lost her mind," said Cleebo.

"She evermore has," said Boon.

"Good garden of peas," said Ruby. She stood up, swiped

dust from her overalls, and shoved her hair out of her face. "My mama didn't sign me up! I'm dancing outta here."

"Me, too!" said Cleebo.

"Your mama's gonna whup you good if you leave, Cleebo!" said Wilkie Collins, first baseman. He peered at Cleebo through thick glasses. "She signed you up just like mine did!"

Cleebo kicked the dirt. A puff of dust drifted over his shoe. He motioned to his teammates sitting in the shade under the chinaberry tree. "Who's with me? Let's get out of here!"

Finesse gushed passionate tears as she saw the boys rise. *"Mes danseurs!"* she said, holding her arms out as if she were offering them the world. *"Mes danseurs ballet!"*

"Not on your life!" said Cleebo. "House!"

House squinted at Finesse in the high-morning glare. The time had come. He tried to sound calm. "I came to bring Honey. The team came with me. We're leaving now."

The news struck Finesse like a collapsed lung. She clapped her hand to her chest and staggered backward one step. "You mean . . . you're not staying? You're not going to . . . help?"

"We don't dance," said House. He made it up as he went along. He put Honey down, retrieved his sunglasses, and shoved them onto the brim of his cap in one smart gesture and repeated himself. "We don't dance. We play ball."

"Ball?" asked Finesse, ready for the volley. *"Le base-ball?"* She made a *tsk-tsk-tsk!* sound. "Don't tell me you still put together that little *ragamuffin* sandlot team every summer?" She straightened her shoulders as if she were royalty. "Honestly, House, at some point one must grow beyond running around after a silly white ball!"

A bitter taste burped itself up from House's gullet and he spit it into the dirt. If he'd had a silly white ball, he'd have thrown it at Finesse's silly propellered head with pleasure. *Plop!* One toad down, just like a carnival game! Instead he threw a few more words, which amazed him, as he was unaccustomed to throwing around words in public. But the circumstances were dire. "We got to go."

Finesse sniffed and tried her best to look regal.

"Don't leave me, House!" Honey clung to her brother's leg. She stared at Finesse with a tinge of terror in her eyes. "I don't think she is who you think she is!"

"You've got a part, Honey," said House. "You're a dancer." Honey sniffed and wiped her eyes. House whistled and Eudora Welty struggled to her old feet, her tutu wobbling around her neck and her tiny tongue hanging out of her mouth. She snorted, wagged her tail tepidly, and blinked into the bright sun beyond the chinaberry tree.

"Let's go," said House.

Finesse rifled through the papers on her clipboard.

"I'll come, too!" called Ruby over the heads of a half-dozen others. She vaulted over Melba, Violet, and Melba's little brother, George. "I'll just run get my glove—"

"No girls allowed," House said. He flexed his pitching hand.

"But I know baseball!" sputtered Ruby. "And I'm eleven! Almost as old as you! I'm good! Cleebo can tell you, he's played catch with me a million times!"

"I don't know what you're talking about," said Cleebo. He wore his most indignant look, which, for Cleebo, meant he looked totally guilty.

Honey's eyes filled with tears. "Do I get tap shoes, House?"

"Sure you do," said House. He took his sister's hand. "Let's go." His voice held a softness he reserved for Honey alone. "I'll bet it's lunchtime by the time we get home."

"Aw, House!" cried Cleebo. "We ain't got all day!"

"I'll catch up," said House. "Start without me."

Finesse tore a piece of paper from her clipboard and waved it in the air like it was on fire. "None of you is going anywhere!" she snapped in perfect, high-pitched English. "Nobody moves!"

Honey shrieked. So did Violet and George. Eudora Welty plopped herself right back into the dirt, stuck her snout between her paws, and shivered.

"All of you!" barked Finesse. "*Tout le monde!* You'll stay right here! You're all on my list!"

Tout le monde sucked in its collective breath.

Finesse straightened her shoulders with an exaggerated move and pruned up her face. "I've got *you* on my list, Ruby Lavender! I've got *you*, House Jackson!" She stabbed her finger at the back row: "And all your little ballplayers, too!"

Baseball is reassuring. It makes me feel as if the world is not going to blow up.
—Sharon Olds, *This Sporting Life*

Honey sniffed back her tears. The sound caught Finesse's attention. Her face softened. With great ceremony, while the sun baked the day and even the breeze stood still as a statue, Finesse took a handkerchief from her tote bag and dotted it around her face.

"Do forgive me, *mes amis,*" she said. "It's the heat—*il fait chaud.* And, it's my passion! I care so much about this pageant, and we have scarcely two weeks to prepare for the production on Independence Day! I have been charged with such great responsibility!"

House spit into the dirt at his feet. Cleebo spit in solidarity with House. Ballplayers standing at the back of the crowd spit. Ruby spit. There was a momentary spitting party.

"Let's take a moment to regroup, *mes amis*!" said Finesse. She fanned her face with her handkerchief. "In fact, let's all take a moment to breathe. Breeeeathe!" She stretched her arms over her head. "A little yoga, perhaps, to bring us back to center?" She gestured in Ruby's direction. "Sit! Sit!"

Ruby rolled her eyes and did as she was told. George tugged on Ruby's overalls. "I thought your mama didn't sign you up," he whispered.

"Miss Mattie signed her up," said Melba. "Now hush."

Cleebo slid himself along the trunk of the chinaberry tree and plopped onto the dirt and berries underneath. The creases on his jeans were all but gone.

"Your mama's gonna whup you with them stained pants," said Wilkie.

"Are you speakin' from experience?" asked Cleebo. "My mama ain't never whupped me in her life."

"I'm just saying," said Wilkie. "Everybody knows she likes her laundry just so . . ."

Several ballplayers began the Sunshine Laundry chant. Cleebo groaned and rested his head on his crossed arms.

Finesse clapped her hands. "Come to order, *mes amis*! Time to get to work!"

House lowered himself to the earth next to Cleebo at

the trunk of the chinaberry tree. Honey dropped like a wilted little leaf into her brother's lap. Next to them, Eudora Welty panted and snuffled.

Finesse continued. "Our play will emanate from within! We will decide together its shape! To help us decide, we will incorporate relaxation techniques, basic sensory and imagination exercises... In short, we will experience a *renaissance*—a rebirth!—of the art of the organic playmaking tradition! We will honor Aurora County—a county full of American towns!—on America's birthday! We will celebrate our wonderful past and our glorious present! Every detail of our lives here in Aurora County is important—*im-por-tant!*"

She took a deep breath and smiled broadly at Honey. "For instance," she said, "you want to dance... and it's coming to me... Let me see..." She put the back of her hand to her head and did a small fainting backward move, then righted herself. "Yes! I've got it! How do you feel about the Dance of the Moon Pie Fairy?" she asked. "I can see it now..."

Honey sat up straight and spoke with great hope in her voice: "Does she wear tap shoes?" She leaned forward to hear the verdict.

"Fairies wear wings and sparkles," said Finesse with finality, "... and they dance barefoot."

Honey burst into tears. Finesse clasped her hands under

her chin and gave Honey an asphyxiated look. "Pleeease don't cry! You must learn to trust my direction!" Honey sobbed while Finesse babbled on.

Eudora Welty crept on her belly toward Honey and snuffled her snout into Honey's lap. House patted on both the dog and his sister. Maybe he could strangle Finesse later. He glared at her as she postured in front of everyone, like she was a queen bee and they were her drones. She'd probably live to be older than Mr. Norwood Boyd—she'd probably live to be a hundred.

"We're sinking like the *Titanic*," moaned Cleebo. "Now what?"

Finesse lifted one leg and pointed her toe for effect as she demonstrated various modern dance possibilities.

"I wanted...wanted...to be a tap dancer, House," Honey whispered to her brother in jagged little hiccups. "I don't want...want...to be in this pageant."

"Everything's going to be all right, Honey," said House. He gave Honey to Cleebo, who patted on a patch of grass under the chinaberry tree. Honey and Eudora both crowded onto it and rested their weary spirits. House rose to his feet.

"Look, Frances." He interrupted Finesse's discourse on the benefits of unscripted skits and spontaneous combustion dialogue.

"Excusez-moi?"

Now that he was standing there, he cast about for

something to say. "We're melting out here—let's go into the schoolhouse—"

Finesse shook her head. "There's *construction* in there! We're not allowed inside."

Melba Jane raised her hand.

"A question!" said Finesse, delight in her voice.

Melba swallowed. "Is it true that the new stage will have footlights?"

"Mais oui!" chirped Finesse. "The new stage will be shiny! It will have footlights! An enormous spotlight! Working microphones! And more!"

Melba's face radiated happiness and Finesse seized the moment while she had it. "I remember you, Melba Jane—you sing in the operetta every August! You have the theater in your blood, *mon ami*! Come stand with me. I dub you my Sancho Panza. I will be your Don Quixote!"

"Really?" Melba whispered.

"Don't do it, Melba," said Ruby. "We don't know those guys!"

But Melba rose, entranced, and floated toward her Don Quixote.

★ 7 ★

To have great poets,
there must be great audiences too.
—Walt Whitman

"Your first task is to take the roll each time we meet." Finesse handed the clipboard to Melba, who took it as if she were handling a newborn baby.

"I want off the list!" barked Cleebo. "I'm the best first baseman in the state of Mississippi, and the Aurora County All-Stars got a game on the Fourth of July! It's our onliest game and we ain't gonna give it up!"

"You're a catcher!" said Ruby. Cleebo ignored her.

"Your mama is one of Dr. Dan Deavers's biggest fans, Cleebo Wilson," said Melba in a cool, take-charge voice. "She's not going to let you off the list. She and half the Mamas watch *Each Life Daily Turns* from the front room of the Sunshine Laundry every afternoon while Lurleen learns how to iron with that new pressing machine."

"That's what's wrong with your head," said Wilkie. "Sleepin' on all that starch!"

Cleebo shoved Wilkie. Wilkie shoved him back. Finesse smiled and nodded at Melba. Melba marked Cleebo present, marked herself present, then began calling out the name of every person on the list.

There were twenty-one names on the list. Eight of them were ballplayers. All of them were under fourteen, all signed up for the 200th anniversary children's pageant representing the wonders of tiny Aurora County, founded on the now-defunct fortunes of an old sawmill in the piney woods of southern Mississippi, where the accents were so thick that words such as *here* and *now* were pronounced in two syllables, where folks said *y'all* and *yonder* every day, and where everyone drank sweet tea and ate sliced tomatoes at every midday meal. And where it was so hot in June, you could fry an egg on the sidewalk. If you had a sidewalk.

"I'm afraid you have no choice!" chirped Finesse. "And just think—you get to meet my uncle! *Mon oncle!* Dr. Dan Deavers of *Each Life Daily Turns*! The man who is making this pageant possible! This is a once-in-a-lifetime opportunity! We'll have a rigorous schedule for the next two weeks, in order to be ready on July Fourth..."

"Nope!" House felt the word leave his gut with way too much breath behind it. It rushed out, strident, high, and uncontrolled, but it would not be denied—it was time to swallow his toad.

He shoved his sunglasses onto his face. "We've got us a ball game on the Fourth of July at four o'clock." He looked from face to face. They were all staring at him like he was on display. His nerve began to evaporate—he reached for something else to say before it vanished completely. "I missed that game last year—*Frances.*" There. He said what everyone knew, and as soon as he said it, it held no power over him. He held the power. He made himself as tall as he could. When he spoke, his voice was strong and straight. "I missed that game last year—*Frances*—and I'm not gonna miss it again!" He checked himself over mentally. He felt marvelous. He was practically radiating.

"Now you're talkin'!" said Cleebo. Honey and Eudora had both fallen asleep. Cleebo scrambled to his feet and pointed at Finesse, who was dotting a handkerchief on her forehead. "We lost that game last year because of you!" he shouted. "You! And don't you think for one minute we ain't gonna win it back this year! If you do, you got another think coming!" Cleebo was so mad, his face turned a puffed-up purple—he looked like an angry eggplant. The rest of the All-Stars clambered to their feet, shouting their agreement. Little kids recoiled from Cleebo as if he might explode.

"You nearly killed House here!" spit Cleebo. "You..." His words gargled in his throat, strangling him. "I need a drink!"

And, as if he'd been released from prison and could now do whatever he wanted to do, Cleebo made a beeline for the schoolhouse where, in great, round sweeps, he unwound the hose from its position on the back wall.

Drunk on the power of his own words, House made like a hornet after Cleebo. "Good idea!" He snatched the end of the hose and marched with it the few feet back to the crowd. Finesse stared at him with eyes as round as Moon Pies. House pointed the end of the hose directly at Finesse. He called over his shoulder to Cleebo: "Turn it on!" No one moved.

Cleebo blinked. "What?"

"Turn it on!"

It took Cleebo two seconds to understand. "All right!" He turned the spigot on full strength. House crimped the hose in his fist to keep the water from spraying out. He aimed the nozzle at Finesse's propellered head. "It's hot out here," he said. Water dripped onto the ground from the end of the hose.

"You wouldn't dare!" said Finesse.

Kids scrambled to their feet and scattered, all but Honey, who continued to snore, out of the line of fire, with her head on top of Eudora Welty under the chinaberry tree. Everyone watched from a safe distance, as if they were all cowboys witnessing the gunfight at the OK Corral. House was armed with a hose. Finesse had a clipboard. There was no contest.

House felt more alive than he'd felt in a whole year. He trained the hose at the face of the girl who had almost ruined his baseball career. The ball team gathered around him.

"We're the Aurora County All-Stars," he said in a voice so calm it surprised him. "We're gonna play baseball on the Fourth of July, and we're leaving."

"Yeah," said Wilkie, his eyes on House. "We're leavin'!"

"Yeah!" said the ball team, full of admiration for their leader.

"You . . . you can't leave," said Finesse. Her voice cracked.

"Watch us!" shouted House. "The ball field is just over yonder—right field backs up to the schoolyard, you can see it from here!" He lifted the hose to eye level and sighted Finesse like a target.

This would have been a good time to shut up, but Finesse couldn't stop herself. "You're . . . you're signed up!"

House squeezed the hose until his whole left arm hurt, which made him even angrier. "I feel our departure emanating from within!" he shouted, plunging ahead. "But before we go, I have a *basic sensory exercise* for you, full of *wonderful past and glorious present*!" He thrust the hose toward Finesse like it was the sword of the rightful king, come to smite her. With his free hand he fixed his thumb over the opening. As he began to release the kink, water sizzled and made a puddle at his feet.

Finesse snatched her straw tote and held it against her sequined shirt like a shield. She stepped backward. "I *know* you are a gentleman, House Jackson."

The summer locusts screamed from the trees. Kids froze at attention in the blazing summer heat.

"Git her, House!" snarled Cleebo. "You know her—she ain't gonna let this go. She'll call everybody's mamas and tell on us. They'll make us do it, and we don't got no time for a pageant! She ain't gonna let us alone. Go on, House—git her!"

The great thing about baseball is
that there's a crisis every day.
—Gabe Paul, general manager, Cincinnati Reds

House sucked in a giant breath of hot summer air, the way he did whenever he wound up for a big pitch. But instead of envisioning his pitch going straight across the plate—*strike!*—or instead of envisioning the water from the hose hitting its mark—*splat!*—instead, the image of Mr. Norwood Rhinehart Beauregard Boyd lying on the cold metal embalming table at Snowberger's Funeral Home, dead, without his glasses, maybe without his clothes, covered with a white sheet, slid into his mind. His anger wheezed and sputtered.

House shook his head to clear it.

Finesse shook her head back at House.

And that's when the sound of tires rolling over pebbles

on the dirt road diverted everyone's attention. Bunch Snowberger drove his black hearse right up to the empty lot behind the school, right up to the pageant players.

House stared at the hearse as his heart began a frantic bang against his rib cage. His face sizzled like it might dissolve right in front of everybody. They were coming for him. They'd ask him a bunch of questions. He'd be found out. He clutched harder at the kink in the hose to make sure he didn't let it get away from him.

Bunch Snowberger opened the back door of the hearse and out stepped Parting Schotz, Finesse's great-grandfather. At his full height, he was no taller than House. He had a stubbly sprinkle of silver gray hair across the back of his head and skin the color of the pinecones that dotted the forest floor. He wore his barber apron; he had come straight from work.

House blinked, as if clearing his vision would help him understand what was happening.

"Poppy?" Finesse's face was a mixture of relief and distress.

Pip—for that's what everyone in town had called Parting Schotz all his life—Pip grabbed Finesse's elbows with his slender, strong hands and gave off one great shuddery sob. Then he gestured toward the hearse.

"Come on, sugar. We need the family together now."

Finesse didn't wait for explanations. She didn't even say good-bye and good luck. She popped into the car with her great-grandfather before you could say *What happened?*—she didn't even glance at her subjects. Bunch clicked the door shut behind them and drove the car away.

House stared at his hands still clenching the hose. They shook like trees in a storm.

"Wow!" said Evan Evans as he watched the hearse disappear. "That was some getaway."

"Somebody's dead," said Ruby.

"It's got to be somebody who's kin to Finesse," said Wilkie.

"That could be a hundred people around here," said Cleebo.

"Somebody run to Miss Mattie's store and find out who died," said Melba, waving the clipboard for an *I'm in command* effect.

"I'll go," said Ruby, "and not because you say so." She ran across the field and toward the row of stores on Main Street.

House began to cough. He unkinked the hose and let the water splat and spray into the dust. He took off his baseball cap, stuck his face into the stream of cold water, then shook the wetness from his head. "Who wants a drink?" he asked in a robotic voice. Finally. He could speak. He handed the hose to whoever would take it first. Wilkie took it gingerly from his hands.

Kids eyed House cautiously as they milled around the hose, drinking or waiting for a turn. They were hot, cranky, and confused. Honey, lost in a dream, draped her arm over Eudora and sighed.

"Are we practicing or not, House?" asked Cleebo. He jittered like he had ants in his pants.

"It's too hot," said House. He took the hose and handed it to Cleebo, who slurped at the stream of water, then spit into the dirt and wiped a wet hand across his face. His jeans were splotched with mud from the nearby puddle and his crisply starched T-shirt was streaked with dirt. "We play no matter what—it's in the rules! You wanna beat them Redbugs or what?"

"We'll beat 'em." House picked up his slumbering sister. Eudora Welty wobbled herself to a puddle and began to slurp. Honey tucked her head under her brother's chin. House said, "I gotta take Honey home."

"Hey!" came a shout from across the lot. "I know who it is!" Ruby hollered. "I know who died!"

Nothing can happen
more beautiful than death.
—Walt Whitman

Ruby grabbed the hose from Cleebo and drank like she was dying of thirst. Then she made her announcement. Water dripped off her chin and her eyes were wide in astonishment. "It's Mr. Norwood Boyd! Mean-Man Boyd!"

Cleebo popped like a firecracker. "Baby-Eater Boyd?"

Ruby nodded. "Can you believe it?"

House swayed, wandlike, at the words. Honey began to wake up in his arms.

"We went by his house this morning!" said Cleebo importantly. "I knew it! I knew somethin' had happened! There's a mess of kudzu all over the place, like they had to hack it down to get in there!"

The news crackled the air like thunder.

"Are you sure?" asked Melba. "Finesse can't be related to him!"

"How do you know?" said Ruby.

"Who is Mean-Man Boyd?" asked George Latham, who was only five.

Ruby spoke with every twist of the spigot as she turned off the hose. "Meanest . . . man . . . who ever . . . drew . . . a breath . . . of life."

"Rich, too," said Wilkie.

"Yeah," said Cleebo, a glint in his eye. "He hoarded trunks full of treasure in that old rattrap of a house, from all them years he traveled all over the world." Cleebo rubbed his hands together in a greedy gesture and stared, bug-eyed, at the kids. "Treasure! Just sittin' there, waiting for somebody to come find it."

Kids nodded. It was a well-worn tale. Mr. Norwood Rhinehart Beauregard Boyd the Merchant Marine who came back from his world travels only to hole up in his house for the past twenty years—alone. No one even knew what he looked like anymore.

House's stomach flip-flopped. He whistled for Eudora.

"Why is he the meanest man?" asked George in a timid voice, as if he couldn't help it and had to know, even if he might be sorry.

"He kidnapped kids and they were never heard from again!" said Boon Tolbert.

"He ate 'em!" said his brother Ned, only too happy to add to the story.

"That's ridiculous," said Melba, halfheartedly, draping her arms around George and Violet both and shooting daggers at Cleebo. "He couldn't get away with that."

"Oh-yes-he-could!" crowed Cleebo. "And did! For years! How do you think he got food to eat? The ghosts of all those dead kids he kidnapped still live in that old place, and there's tons of 'em—he's hundreds of years old! He comes back to life every time he dies!"

"Eeeeeee!" squealed George and Violet and every other pageant kid under ten.

"Stop it!" shouted House. He put Honey down. She buried her face in his leg. She was sticky with sweat.

"What do you care?" asked Cleebo. Eudora Welty stood next to House, wagging her tail and looking droopy. Cleebo stared at the dog, then at House. He began connecting the dots. "What do you care?" he asked House again. "Unless you know somethin' we don't?"

House cleared his throat. "You're scaring Honey."

Honey nodded into House's leg. Her tutu was crushed.

Across the empty lot, walking with a purposeful gait, came Miss Mattie Perkins, Ruby's aunt and owner of the mercantile. She wore a flour sack apron and had her hair pinned into a no-nonsense bun on the back of her head.

"What's happening here?" she needled. "Is it a convention?"

Ruby's face reddened to the color of her hair. "I was just tellin' them about Mean...I mean, Mr. Norwood Boyd..."

"I figured you were." Miss Mattie put her hands on her hips, pursed her lips, and stared at everyone until each kid fidgeted. "Time to go home, all of you," she said. "There will be practice here in the morning, nine o'clock sharp, for every name on the pageant list." Her gaze speared each ballplayer's face and each one looked somewhere else. "Remember," she said, "if your mama signed you up, you show up. This pageant is not only a tribute to the county, it's a thank-you to Frances's uncle for his generosity in supplying us with the new stage. The pageant will go on as scheduled...on July Fourth at four o'clock at Halleluia School."

Cleebo elbowed House. House ignored him. No one protested to Miss Mattie. "Now, go home," she said. "It's hot. You'll get an earlier start tomorrow."

"Miss Mattie," said Melba. "Is Mr. Norwood Boyd kin to Finesse...er, Frances?"

Miss Mattie carefully untied and retied the strings on her apron and said, "Norwood Boyd had no family." She let her breath out slowly. "Rest his soul."

Rest his soul. The words were so final—they grabbed House by the throat. He swallowed hard. The thought of crying in front of everyone horrified him. He took a deep breath, and held it.

"Then why . . . ," Ruby began.

"How did he die?" asked George. His face was a mixture of wonder and horror.

House was light-headed, still holding his breath.

"I don't know, child," said Miss Mattie. "But we'll soon find out all about it."

We'll soon find out all about it. With no warning, House's knees buckled beneath him. He sank like a ship and landed in the dirt, just missing Eudora Welty. Honey shrieked.

Miss Mattie grabbed House by the arm and pulled him up. "What's wrong with you, House? You're white as a ghost!"

House blinked and licked his lips. "Hot."

Cleebo was ever-ready with a reply. "He's out of his head with heat," he said hastily. "I'll get him home." He fanned House with his baseball cap. "C'mon, buddy. Let's go."

House waved him away. "I'm fine." He stood and brushed the dust off his jeans.

"Suit yourselves," said Miss Mattie. "Cleebo, if you can't find something constructive to do, go help your mama at the laundry; Lurleen's out today."

"Yes'm," said Cleebo. "I got to get House home first."

Miss Mattie harrumphed and walked back to the mercantile with Ruby and Melba reluctantly in tow. "I've got work for you girls. I need help until Eula returns from her trip."

The energy fizzled out of the day. Kids wandered toward home, talking in little groups of twos and threes. The drama of the morning was over. Honey took House's hand and gave him a quizzical look.

"I'm hungry," said Wilkie. "Let's practice later." The team murmured a tentative approval.

"House can't play later," said Boon.

Ned nodded. "Yeah, he can only play after supper until dark, remember?"

Cleebo clapped a hand on House's pitching shoulder as if he'd been empowered to arrest him. "You comin' to practice this afternoon, House?"

House pulled his shoulder away from Cleebo's grasp. The idea of his newfound freedom hadn't occurred to him until now. He scooped at the hot summer air with an empty overhand pitch. "Four o'clock. I'm pitching aspirin tablets! Get ready."

Cleebo raised an eyebrow but didn't comment.

"'Bout time we had some fastballs!" said Boon. "You've been throwin' dead mackerels for weeks."

"Yeah! Let's get ready for those Redbugs!" said Lincoln and Arnold and Evan. "Finally!"

House gave Eudora another little whistle. "Let's go, girl."

"That's the ugliest dog I ever saw," said Cleebo. "Dogs are supposed to be houndy with floppy tongues."

"This one isn't," said House.

"YouDoggie is beautiful," Honey said simply.

And with that, the baseball team disbanded for the duration of the hot day. The empty lot was left to the grasshoppers and the soon-to-come shadows and secrets of late afternoon.

WBAC

IN BEAUTIFUL AURORA COUNTY
YOUR STATION FOR LOCAL NEWS AND WEATHER!

RADIO FLASH NEWS!

Composed and Read by Phoebe "Scoop" Tolbert
June 17, noon

Lord-a-mercy, here's a tidbit of breaking news from the Halleluia Bureau. It has just occurred to this reporter that the annual Aurora County All-Stars Game, which is always played on July 4 at 4pm, is scheduled to take place at the same time as the once-in-a-lifetime Aurora County Birthday Pageant, funded by Dr. Dan Deavers of Our Fair County. (Dr. Dan is having a new stage constructed at Halleluia School expressly for this purpose!)

Now. The ball game is sparsely attended, this is true, and it is the only official game our boys get to play each year, against the Smith County Raleigh Redbugs, who are also too few in number to warrant an official Little League team. But it is an important event! My grandsons, the Tolbert twins, are beside themselves with worry over the fact that they will miss their game, especially after last year's loss—they want a chance to redeem themselves! They have refused to eat their vegetables until there is a resolution!

The time and date of the ball game cannot be moved—families from both Aurora and Smith counties set this date aside each year to picnic and play this game and there is no other good time when we can congregate.

The pageant time and date cannot be moved. Aurora County was founded on the Fourth of July, and Dr. Dan cannot leave his soap opera to be in attendance at any other time, due to the fact that he has come out of his coma on the show, and is making his comeback from the amnesia.

What will this mean for the pageant? For the game? Mamas? Papas? How do we proceed?

This is Phoebe Tolbert, the Vivacious Voice of Aurora County, signing off until next time!

I don't make speeches.
I just let my bat speak for me in the summertime.
—HONUS WAGNER, SHORTSTOP, PITTSBURGH PIRATES

Cleebo, House, Honey, and Eudora Welty walked down the middle of the dirt road, a road that traveled the almost-mile from Halleluia to Mabel. Mabel was a crossroads dotted with farms, scattered with homes, and blessed with two large churches that faced each other across a dirt road, and a county middle school that boasted a brand-new woodworking shop and greenhouse.

The sun beat down on the travelers like a hot gold hammer.

"I ain't never seen you like that, House," said Cleebo.

"Like what?"

"Standin' up to Frances!"

"What do you mean?"

"I mean, I never saw you do that before!"

"Do what?"

"Approach your problems! You never *approach* your problems, House. You don't talk about 'em—"

"You talk enough for the both of us—," House interrupted, but Cleebo bulldozed on.

"—and that's what gets folks in trouble—they don't approach their problems."

"Where'd you learn to talk like that? Your problem is you've been watching that soap opera at the laundry."

"I can't help that—it's on when I'm there for lunch. I'm tellin' you, House, sometimes things need *approaching*."

"I approach the plate. That's enough." But he had approached his problem, and he knew it. He had survived it, too.

Cleebo punched his fist into his catcher's mitt for effect. "You moused around all last summer after you got your elbow broke. I woulda gone after Frances right then and there!" He shoved his hands into his pockets and slouched toward home. "You shoulda blasted Frances just now, House. She deserves it."

House worked his elbow. "I think the arm's fine" was all he said. He tossed his baseball in the air and caught it.

Cleebo kicked a rock in front of him. "So you can play ball in the afternoons now, House? What gives?"

"Nothin' gives."

Cleebo hooted. "All year long, the whole team showed

up to play ball after school and you said you couldn't come. School got out and still you only showed up in the evenin's. Now you can come anytime? I'm your best friend and you ain't gonna tell me why?"

"Nope."

"I don't know about you, House. We've had to do without you with no good explanation—I've been mighty forgiving about it..."

"My arm was broke half the time!"

"It's not broke now!"

"Well, here I am!" House shouted. "Let's play!" It felt good to yell.

Cleebo yelled, too. "We ain't gonna have a game if we don't figure out this pageant problem!"

"Well, I don't have answers right now, Cleebo! Why do *I* have to figure out all the answers?"

"Because you're team captain! It's your team! You put it together in the first place!"

House sidestepped Eudora Welty, who was wobbling her back-and-forth gait.

"Hey!" said Honey. "Be careful!"

"Where'd your dog come from?" asked Cleebo.

"Found her in the bushes," said House.

"I love her!" chirped Honey, who was struggling to keep up. "Her name is YouDoggie!"

"Eudora," said House.

"That's what I said," said Honey. "YouDoggie!"

Cleebo and House rounded a curve in the road.

"Looka here!" burst Cleebo.

The gates to Mr. Norwood Boyd's house were open.

"Wow...," breathed Cleebo, staring at the crumbling house beyond the gates. "It's Mean-Man's house..."

"Yeah...," House spoke in his most noncommittal voice.

He shoved his hands in his pockets. There was his note, still rolled into a small, crunched scroll.

Cleebo squinted at House. "You knew Baby-Eater Boyd."

"What are you talking about?" House looked behind him for Honey.

"You knew him," said Cleebo. "I can tell."

House shook his head. "Nah."

"Yeah, you did," said Cleebo. "It got to you, all that talk about him dyin' and who he was."

"You know what, Cleebo? You talk too much! I wish you'd catch as good as you talk."

"What are you talking about? I'm a good catcher!"

At that moment, Honey and Eudora caught up to the boys. Eudora Welty stopped short, sniffed the air, then ran straight through the open gate to Norwood Boyd's house and disappeared.

"YouDoggie!" screamed Honey.

"Eudora!" House sprinted after the dog with Cleebo on his heels.

"Don't go in there, House!" screamed Honey.

House and Cleebo screeched to a halt at the gate. "Eudora!" House called. The dog was gone. "Let me get her, Honey."

"No! There's ghosts in there!" cried Honey. She pulled on her brother's shirt as hard as she could.

"There's no such thing," said House. "That's just a story . . ."

"Nooooo!" Honey began to cry. She leaned forward and wailed for Eudora. "YouDoggie!"

Cleebo hissed. "I see where that dog comes from, and I know you know somethin'. You can tell me. What did you do to him? Did you find the treasure?"

"You're crazy, Cleebo!" House wrapped his arms around Honey, who was hollering herself blue for Eudora.

"She's in there with the ghosts!"

"Ghosts can't see dogs," said House. "And there ain't no ghosts."

"Then why don't you go in and get her?" Cleebo spit into the mountain of kudzu by the gate.

"*You* go!" said House. He stood and glowered at Cleebo. "Go on! You know so all-fired much about ghosts and treasure!"

Cleebo eyeballed the decaying old house and took a step through the driveway gates. Honey screeched. She wrapped her arms around herself like a mummy and held her breath.

Cleebo stepped back.

"You're not as brave as you thought you were," said House. "And there ain't no treasure."

Cleebo jabbed his finger at House. "You know somethin'."

House spit. "I know I'm goin' home."

"YouDoggieeeeee!" Honey wailed.

"She'll be at home waiting for us, Honey. Let's go."

Cleebo took off his baseball cap and wiped his forehead with his sweaty T-shirt. "You really gonna be at practice this afternoon? Or you gonna be *busy*?"

"Let's you and me part company, Cleebo. You can get your bike and go home."

"What about lunch? I bet your daddy is fixin' four, maybe five peanut butter and jelly sandwiches right now..."

"I don't want company!" House took Honey's hand. She made a miserable sound through her tears.

"What am I supposed to do for lunch?"

"I don't care what you do. Go eat with the Mamas at the Sunshine Laundry and watch Dr. Dan on the television. Go get starched, Cleebo."

"Fine!" cried Cleebo. "I don't care if you show up for practice or not!"

"Yes, you do!" House let go of Honey's hand. She collapsed like a sad little balloon that was all out of air. House took an angry step toward Cleebo. The inside of his nose stung with tears. "Watch me *approach* my problems, Cleebo! You tell me every day how I let the team down last year. What kind of friend does that? *I'm* the one that's been forgiving! A broke elbow is a broke elbow!"

Cleebo blinked. "Well, you shoulda watched where you were going!"

House crammed his ball and glove into his armpit. "It wasn't my fault, Cleeb," he said in an even voice.

"You know what, House?" Cleebo took one last look at the gloom that was Norwood Boyd's house. "Eatin' at the laundry's better than eatin' with you any day!" He stalked back toward town, throwing a shout over his shoulder. "I'll get my bike later! Don't you touch it!"

House picked up Honey, who sobbed into her brother's neck. "It'll be all right, Honey."

But it would not be all right. House was wrong.

He was wrong about Eudora.

Wrong about the treasure.

Wrong about everything.

Special Edition, June 17

THE AURORA COUNTY NEWS

SNIPPETS FROM SNOWBERGER'S (An Occasional Column on the Deceased of Aurora County)

Mr. Norwood Rhinehart Beauregard Boyd Claimed by Death Thursday Morn'g!

By Comfort Snowberger: Historian, Recipe Tester, and Funeral Reporter with help from Goldie Shuggars, Snowberger's Resident Archivist

We here at Snowberger's Funeral Home live to serve. We pride ourselves on knowing every body who has died in our county. We keep careful records of all the deceased and their resting places.

So you can imagine the sheer surprise of it all when Bunch Snowberger was called away from his worktable (where he was carefully preparing Mr. Clark Terry for his funeral and eternal rest) to ride Sheriff Taylor over in the hearse to the nearby Mabel home of Mr. Norwood Rhinehart Beauregard

Boyd—a closed-up, veritable haunted house of a place, full of old treasures from long-ago travels and...Mr. Norwood Boyd!

A mysterious phone call alerted Doc MacRee to the death.

"I thought he'd died eons ago!" said Goldie Shuggars, Snowberger's Resident Archivist and (she wants you to know) new to the job.

"I thought he was a *ghost,*" said an amazed Tidings Snowberger, resident yard mower and bush trimmer.

"Heavens! Where and to whom do I send flowers?" said Joy Snowberger, wife of Bunch and mother to little Merry, who took one look at Mr. Norwood Boyd's body as it was wheeled into the Snowberger's workroom and said, simply and affirmatively, "Dead!"

"Folks forgot he was alive," said Bunch Snowberger. "I forgot, too." There was real sadness in his voice.

It is rumored that years ago Mr. Norwood Boyd returned from many years at sea and locked himself up in his house, never to be heard from again. Why? And what happened after that? We may never know.

A letter of direction written in Norwood Boyd's hand was found on the bed next to him. He has requested no funeral and instead sends word that he has other plans, although they have not as yet been discovered or disclosed. We here at Snowberger's await any forthcoming news so we can figure out what to do. If anyone is kin to Norwood Boyd, please contact Snowberger's immediately. (We have a new batch of oversized Snowberger's handkerchiefs—now being laundered and ironed by the all-new Sunshine Laundry!—in baskets placed strategically around the Serenity Suite, so don't worry about tears when you come forth to tell your story. We've got you covered.)

As always, Snowberger's remains a place of family comfort and repose. When you arrive for your loved one's funeral you can rest assured that your every need will be attended to from the moment the door is opened by our greeter, Peach Shuggars ("So glad to SEE you!"), to the moment you are ready to depart, when our new puppy, Surprise Snowberger, walks (runs, twirls, jumps, yips) with you to your car to see you safely home.

I believe a leaf of grass is no less than
the journey-work of the stars.
—Walt Whitman

Eudora Welty did not come home. Honey would not be comforted and finally fell asleep in her father's lap in a rocker on the front porch. House sat on the porch swing and listened to the chain creak as he rocked himself back and forth.

An afternoon breeze tugged at the corners of the porch and thunder grumbled in the distance. "Thunder makes me think of your mama," his father said. "Seems like every time it rained, she had sheets hanging on the line."

"I remember," said House.

"You do?" His father shifted Honey in his lap.

"We pulled the sheets off the line in the rain," said House. "We laughed."

"We sure did," said his father. "Those were the days." He sighed. "How was the pageant practice?"

"Terrible. The whole team's signed up by their mamas and the game is on the same day. Cleebo thinks I'm supposed to fix it, but I can't. And Frances—she's worse than ever."

His father nodded as if he were processing all this information carefully. "Can nothing be done about the date?"

House shook his head no.

"It would be a shame not to play your game," said his father.

House scratched at his cheek. "I don't know what to do about it."

His father watched the dark clouds move in. "Your mama loved baseball," he said. "Do you still have that glove she gave you just before she died?"

"Yessir."

"I thought Honey might use it one day, but she seems to have other ambitions," said his father.

Thunder crackled its way across the gray sky and House looked over at the empty clothesline. "Is there going to be a funeral for Mr. Norwood?"

"I don't believe he wanted one," said his father. "That's what Pip told me today when I was in town."

"Oh."

"It seems strange to die and not have anyone mark the occasion, doesn't it?" said his father.

"Yessir." House had marked the occasion. He had been there.

The wind rattled the pecans in the trees. The hidden sun cast the yard in a rosy-edged, silver glow. "You did well this past year, son," said his father.

"Yessir."

"I know you didn't want to do it."

"Nossir." He had gotten used to it, though. He had gotten good at sitting by the bedside of a quiet old man. "It wasn't bad, once I got used to it."

"I know," said his father. "I could tell."

Leonard Jackson stood up with the sleeping Honey in his arms. "We're going to get a soaker," he said. "Why don't you lie down for a while, too? You were up half the night."

"We got practice this afternoon," said House.

"Not in a thunderstorm," said his father.

"Maybe it'll pass," said House.

"Maybe," said his father.

"Is Frances related to Mr. Norwood Boyd?"

"Can't say as she is." The sky darkened and lightning flashed in the distance, followed by another low rumble.

"Eudora's at Mr. Norwood's house for sure," said House. "And she's afraid of storms."

"We'll go get her if she doesn't come back," said his father. "She'll be all right."

"Are you staying home?" House scratched a mosquito bite on his elbow.

"Can't mow in the rain," said his father. "I'll tinker in the shed. I've got sandwiches in the kitchen if you want 'em."

Rain dotted the dirt by the pecan trees, setting off a dusty, sleepy smell. House stopped in his bedroom to get the shoe box of baseball cards he'd found on the front porch after his elbow had been set in a cast for the second time, after it had been determined that the break was worse than they'd thought.

No one knew where the box had come from. House had asked his father, Cleebo, the boys, but none of them knew. He and Cleebo had spent hours on rainy days poring over the well-loved, beat-up cards. They memorized statistics, pretended to be one player and then the next, but it was Sandy Koufax—a lefty, like House—who had captured House's imagination. House had even gone to the Bay Springs Library to look up more about Sandy Koufax. Miss Dena DeRose, the librarian, had found articles from old *Life* magazines to share with House. House knew all about Koufax. He felt close to him.

Now while the thunder grumbled to the coming rain and the breeze cooled the afternoon, House sat on his sleeping-porch bed and pulled out cards at random: several

Willie Mays, a slew of Mickey Mantle, three Roger Maris, and on it went—Jackie Robinson, Don Drysdale, Roberto Clemente, Whitey Ford, giants of baseball from years past. He pulled out a Koufax card and stared at that serious face, then turned the card over to reread the statistics he had memorized.

Sandy Koufax had pitched that perfect game in 1965. A perfect game. No runs, no hits, no errors. Each hitter came to the plate, swung, and struck out, one after another until the game was won. Sandy had pitched four career no-hitters. He led the National League in shutouts three times, in strikeouts four times, in wins three times. He made six All-Star appearances, won the National League Most Valuable Player Award in 1963, was World Series MVP twice—once in 1963, and again in that golden year of 1965's perfect game.

House stretched out on the bed and closed his eyes as he listened to the katydids call from the pines. Their insistent summer song melted into a dream and became the songlike voice of Vin Scully announcing from the Dodger Stadium press box: *On the mound tonight for the Los Angeles Dodgers . . . number thirty-two . . . the great left-hander . . . Sandy Koufax!*

And there he was, House, shaking hands with his hero, Koufax. Koufax smiled at House and handed him the baseball. Then he walked to the bench, disappearing with each step. Now House stood on the pitcher's mound alone. He looked up. The stadium was a three-tiered wonder packed with screaming fans. The crowd chanted his name. He could smell the hot dogs, the mustard, the peanuts, the sweat. He tapped the rubber on the mound with the tip of his cleats. He shook out his left arm, his pitching arm—it felt just fine. He clutched the ball in his left hand, gripped the stitches with his fingertips, and looked intently into the glove on his right. He could see every crease in that glove, like a detailed road map of every game he'd ever played.

The roar of the crowd faded and he found himself sitting on the front porch now, back home in Mabel, Mississippi. He was six years old and he had a brand-new glove. He rubbed it with neat's-foot oil, massaging it with both hands, down each finger, the oil smelling like promise, all over his glove. He worked an old baseball into the pocket, turning it around and around, coating it with the oil as well. He could see every stitch in that baseball, every nick. He also saw a name scratched into it: Elizabeth. His mother's name.

She called to him. He tied a string around the glove with the ball in it so it would develop a deep pocket, making it easier to catch the ball. Then he floated, the way bodies do in a dream, off to find his mother.

He smelled the applesauce cake in the kitchen, and he heard his mother singing to herself, singing the song she had sung to House when he was little, the symphony song: *After the dazzle of day is gone,* she sang.

His mother was high in the sky, in the same cirrus clouds he'd seen over Norwood Boyd's house that morning. He joined her, light as a feather and free from all worry. She kissed him right in the middle of his forehead, smiled, and looked deeply into his eyes. He saw her perfectly, for that was the blessing of dreams—he could remember every detail now. The comfort was enormous. House began to cry.

His mother said, *You'll be fine now, House. Remember to listen for the symphony true.*

The symphony! House sprang up in his dream—*I have to tell you!* he began—but his mother dissolved, faded into the cloud, became a hazy memory again. The sky disappeared. House was falling, falling back to Earth and darkness.

★ 12 ★

Life is not a spectator sport. If you're going to spend your whole life in the grandstand just watching what goes on, in my opinion you're wasting your life.

—Jackie Robinson, second baseman, Brooklyn Dodgers

House opened his eyes. It was mud-dark, the time just before full-dark, when the heat of the day fizzed its last and gave way to the cooler, velvet summer night. He lay on his bed on the sleeping porch and listened to the left-over raindrops drip from the pine needles onto the dirt yard. He looked at the clock by the bed. He had slept right through the storm, right through dinner, right through Honey's bedtime. Soon his father would go to bed as well.

He stared at the ceiling, at the lines and cracks in the plaster. His heart beat a steady, strong beat, and it took him a while to come back to himself. He breathed in and out, just as Mr. Norwood Boyd had done that very morning just before daylight. Just as his mother had done six years ago. Just as he would do one day. His father had said, "That day's a long ways off, House, you don't need to worry about that." But sometimes he did.

He didn't need a light to find what he wanted, as the moon was rising early after the rain. The baseball mitt his mother had given him when he was six was on the top shelf in his closet. There. He folded it open, shut, open. He poked his hand into its cool cavern but of course it no longer fit his hand. The smell of neat's-foot oil lingered in the creases. The ball was gone. He couldn't remember why it was gone, or if it had indeed said *Elizabeth*—maybe that was just his dream.

He heard a familiar click and looked down the hall. His father had switched on his reading light. On House's door was taped a note in his father's handwriting:

Cleebo called.
No practice.
Team meets 8am at the Halleluia ball field.
Leftovers in the fridge.

It was time. House left the sleeping porch, careful not to let the screen door slap. The warm night air was damp and alive with the racket of katydids, crickets, and frogs. The moon was a bone white circle. House made his way out to the dirt road, where he walked the half mile to Mr. Norwood Boyd's home. The gate was still open. House went right to the honeysuckle bush beside the front porch. He crawled inside. The wet branches slicked him with leftover rain.

There she was. A little whine, a little lick, a little snuffle. House patted Eudora. "Good dog." He removed the tutu from around her neck and hung it on an inside branch. "Honey loves you," he said. "You could get used to her, you know."

He reached into his pocket and unfolded the note that Eudora Welty had worn around her neck only that morning. When he first read it, he had been stunned. His mother was here, in this note. Moonlight sifted through the honeysuckle branches as House read for the hundredth time the words written with a fountain pen in Norwood Boyd's old-school, perfect handwriting:

After the dazzle of day is gone,
Only the dark, dark night shows to my
eyes the stars.
After the clangor of organ majestic, or
chorus, or perfect band,
Silent, athwart my soul, moves the
symphony true.
—Walt Whitman, Leaves of Grass

His hands shook. There they were, those words of his mother's, her song, the song she had sung so many times, the symphony song. They were written by someone named Walt Whitman. He thought his mother had made them up.

He had forgotten most of the words. It was hard, after all, for a six-year-old to remember or even know what *clangor* meant. What was *athwart*? But *symphony true*—he had remembered that. *After the dazzle of day is gone*—he remembered that. And *the dark, dark night*. Like now. Dark, dark night, with a brilliant moon rising.

Mr. Norwood Boyd had written more:

> *From the library doorway, five bookcases to the right, seventh shelf up, the only green spine.*

He had penned three more lines:

> *Your mother gave these words to me;*
> *Now I give them to you as treasure for the days ahead.*
> *Look for me in every atom that you see.*

House swallowed. None of the words on the page spoke more loudly to him than the knowledge they conveyed: *His mother had known Norwood Boyd.*

He's an old friend of the family, his father had said, *a little peculiar, but nothing to worry about,* he'd said. But this note said more: Elizabeth Jackson had known Norwood Boyd very well.

He shoved the note back into his pocket and stroked Eudora Welty. "Want to go inside, girl?" He led Eudora out of the honeysuckle and together they went around to the back porch, to the door that opened into the summer kitchen, which was a large room with a six-burner stove, a deep enamel sink, and a long wooden table. Ages ago someone canned tomatoes and green beans in this room; ages ago children took baths in here with water that had been heated on the stove and poured into tin tubs sitting on the old wood floor. Maybe one of those children had been Mr. Norwood Boyd—long, long ago.

The summer kitchen hadn't been used in years, much like the rest of the house. Cobwebs drifted from the rafters and the windows were covered in dust. House had never been inside Mr. Norwood Boyd's house alone at night. It was creepy.

He hadn't thought to bring a flashlight, but he knew there was one in Mr. Norwood Boyd's bedroom. He would have to brave the summer kitchen, the dining room, and the wide hallway to get to the front bedroom where Mr. Norwood Boyd had spent most of his time. The library was across the hall from the bedroom. That would be his final destination.

Eudora headed straight for her food and water and began to slurp and crunch. The sounds were comforting, normal.

House took a breath. Took a step. Took another. He tiptoed through the rooms as if there were someone still in the house. As if every atom were alive and watching him.

Down the long, wide hallway he crept until he found himself in front of the door to Mr. Norwood Boyd's bedroom. It was closed. Now that he was faced with turning the knob and walking into the room where Mr. Norwood had died, he couldn't bring himself to go in. He could see well enough in the moonlit dark, he told himself. So he turned around and faced the library door. It, too, was closed. House put his hand on the library doorknob, nervous at another closed door. How many times had he been in this room, finding the next book on Mr. Norwood Boyd's list to be read aloud? And now there was something waiting for him in the library. A treasure.

As he gripped the doorknob and began to turn it, he heard a *click!* behind him from Mr. Norwood Boyd's bedroom door, then the *squeeeeeak!* of the door as it swung wide.

He whirled. A flashlight beam struck him in the eyes and blinded him—he stumbled backward into a narrow table against the hallway wall. A scream gargled in his throat as a hand clapped itself over his mouth.

Someone else's hand.

A cold hand.

A ghost!

Each of us inevitable, each of us limitless—
each of us with his or her right upon the earth.
—WALT WHITMAN

House strangled on his screams. He flailed his arms as if he could shoo away whatever was upon him. He twisted himself away.

"Whoa, son!" It was a man's voice, not a ghost's—a voice alive and strong, breaking through the dark, through the flashlight's beam. House thudded to the floor with a yelp.

"Hush, child!" said the voice. "No need to scream to the high heavens."

Pip! House squinted into the dancing light—now he could see him. Parting Schotz. Frances's great-grandfather. Pip extended a knobby hand to House.

"I . . . I . . ." House tried to think of something to say but his heart was still in his throat and he couldn't breathe.

"Give me your hand," said Pip.

House did as he was told and Pip pulled him to his feet. House sucked in as much air as he could, which set him to coughing. Pip slapped him on the back until he stopped.

"Nobody's going to get you," he said. "What are you doing here, House?"

Eudora Welty trotted down the hallway and blinked at them. House pointed to her. "Dog," he said. "Dog."

Pip called Eudora to him and scratched her back. "I'll bet she's feeling lost."

"Yessir." House tried to breathe slowly. He was light-headed.

"Well," said Pip, "she's used to you being here, so maybe that's a comfort to her right now." He gave Eudora a last pat on the head. "You find Norwood this mornin'?"

House colored up. "Yessir," he said. He willed Pip not to ask him any more questions.

"Thought so," said Pip. "I figured it was you who called it in. What are you doing here now?"

House touched Eudora between her ears. "I figure she needs looking after."

"You going to take her home?" asked Pip.

House shrugged. "I thought I might."

"You come over mighty late."

House concentrated on scratching Eudora's ears. "Yessir." It was all he could think to say while he waited for his heartbeat to return to normal.

Pip persisted, as if he were asking test questions. "Where did you find her?"

"Under the honeysuckle bush," said House.

"But you're in the house..."

"Well..."

Pip nodded. He seemed satisfied. He didn't ask for more. But House did. He asked before he even let himself think about it. "You're in the house, too, Mr. Pip."

"Yes, I am," said Pip. He didn't offer an explanation.

House searched for something to say as Pip stared at him. "You've got real cold hands," he finally said.

"I'm old!" said Pip. "I don't have much heat left in me!"

"You don't?"

"Folks get old and they don't move as much as they used to," said Pip. He hiked up his pants by the belt. "Don't be so shocked! You've seen me here with Norwood when you've come."

"Yessir," said House. "You brought supper..."

"Yes, sometimes I did. That's a fact," said Pip. "But that's not all of it."

House shoved his hands in his pockets. His note was hot, like it was on fire for House to hurry up and do something about it. And here was Pip, about to send him home.

Pip gazed at House thoughtfully, like he was making up

his mind about something. Then he gestured to a place across the hall. "Look here. I'll show you something you haven't seen."

Pip played his flashlight over the walls. Every inch was covered with framed black-and-white photographs. Faces floated into the yellow cone of light and faded away, like ghosts.

"Do you know who these folks are?" Pip asked. House shook his head no.

"Right here," said Pip, pointing to a young black boy wearing a baseball uniform several sizes too large for him. AURORA ANGELS was sewn onto the jersey in a beautiful sky-blue script. It could have spelled out LOS ANGELES DODGERS, as beautifully made as that uniform was.

"This is me!" said Pip. House squinted as Pip steadied the light.

"Don't you wonder about it?" Pip asked.

House nodded. He couldn't take his eyes off the uniform. "We had a Little League team?"

"Somebody did," said Pip, "but there wasn't no 'we' about it."

"You're wearing a uniform," said House.

"It wasn't mine."

"Whose was it?"

"Good question. It was a long time ago." Pip settled into the story. "I was twelve, like you are today. I was the best home run hitter in three counties. And I couldn't play baseball with the Aurora County boys." Pip leaned toward House. "I wasn't allowed."

House could feel Pip's breath on him like a scratchy wool blanket. "Why not?"

Pip sniffed. "I wasn't allowed to play because of the color of my skin," he said in a flat voice. "Just like ol' Satchel Paige—best pitcher who ever lived—wasn't allowed to play in the major leagues, had to stay in the Negro leagues nearly his whole career. I couldn't play with the white boys."

House blinked into Pip's stare. "Really?"

"Really." Pip crossed his arms and the cone of light bobbed along the floor.

"Norwood Boyd was my best friend," Pip continued. "My mama used to work for his mama, and we played together all day long as little boys. But once we started school, we didn't play together anymore. We went to different schools, we had different lives. And we didn't play baseball together, nosirree. That's the way it was then."

"How did you get the uniform?" House whispered.

Pip hitched up his pants. "It was Norwood's. Norwood was a great ballplayer. He was a catcher, as good as Johnny Bench, as good as Josh Gibson, Roy Campanella—did you know that?"

House shook his head—it was unbelievable to think of that old man in the carved rosewood bed as a baseball catcher as good as Johnny Bench.

"Norwood could throw clean from home plate to second and get that runner out," Pip continued. "But I couldn't play with him, nosirree. I couldn't even watch him play, unless I watched from the road. And I was some hitter. I could hit that ball like Ted Williams, like Babe Ruth—I could have been as good as Frank Robinson."

House thought of Cleebo, who loved baseball, whose skin was a darker brown than Pip's. House had been playing ball with Cleebo ever since he could remember.

Pip played the flashlight's beam on the photographs again. "When Norwood got to be twelve, he decided he wouldn't play baseball neither, if I couldn't play. He gave me his uniform."

House and Pip both stared at the photograph in the cone of light. In the photograph, Pip's eyes were crinkled with happiness and an ease seeped out of his pores—you could see it in his stance.

"Norwood took this picture of me in his uniform—took it with his Kodak camera. And for a while we played catch together. Then we quit. The joy went right out of baseball for both of us. I don't know to this day who I felt worse about—me, who couldn't play at all, or Norwood, who refused to play. It didn't make sense."

Pip leaned close to House to make his last point. "Norwood Boyd never again played for a ball team. And you know somethin'?" Pip clapped his hand on House's shoulder. "Norwood was a young boy then. He was full of the fire of living, like all young folks are. Like you are. What would lead a young boy to make a decision like that? To abandon something he loved so much to stand up for someone else?"

"I don't know." House's voice was a whisper.

"Maybe he stood up for himself," said Pip. "Think about it. Maybe he stood up for all of us. Look here."

Pip illuminated photograph after dusty photograph with the flashlight and House took them all in for the first time. Here was young Norwood Boyd, older Norwood Boyd, Norwood Boyd with Parting Schotz, Norwood Boyd with people House didn't know—so many people.

"And when he grew up he joined the Merchant Marines," said Pip. "Just look at everywhere he traveled, at everything he did! Then he ended up in this house alone these past many years, for reasons of his own."

And that was when Pip surprised House: "I loved Norwood Boyd for that one act of friendship. Why did you love him?"

14

I always enjoyed playing ball,
and it didn't matter to me whether I played
with white kids or black. I never understood why
an issue was made of who I played with.
—WILLIE MAYS, CENTER FIELDER, SAN FRANCISCO GIANTS

House's heartbeat thumped in his ears. "I didn't... love him! I didn't know anything about him."

"You visited him every day for one whole year!" said Pip. "And you never found out nuthin' about him?"

"I... I didn't ask him questions."

"Why didn't you, House?"

House thought about it. "Well... he was sick."

Pip nodded his old gray head and stroked his chin with two fingers. "I see. Yes, he was sick. But his mind was good. Where is your sense of wonder, House? You missed the opportunity to know a great man."

They stood in the great man's house in the dark, the silence between them.

House tried to think of a reply. "He scared me at first."

"Folks are scared of what they don't know," said Pip. "What else?"

"My father told me to come," said House. "He said I could be useful to an old man who was going to die soon."

"I know what you did," Pip said. "I set it up with Norwood and then with your daddy."

"You did?"

"I did." The flashlight bobbled along the wall with no particular aim, bouncing like a spotlight on Norwood Boyd's life in pictures as Pip talked. "Doc MacRee spoke with your daddy about it a year ago, when we lost some of our help—my granddaughter Gladys and her family moved to Jackson—you know that story. Doc MacRee and I knew Norwood was going to need more watching over in that gloaming hour before supper and bedtime. Norwood told us you'd be perfect for the job."

"He did?" House fidgeted.

"You're wonderin' why, ain't ya?"

"He didn't even know me."

"He knew you."

"How?"

"Now you got questions!" said Pip. "Now, when it's too late to ask Norwood about 'em!"

"He knew my mother," said House. He'd show Pip he knew something.

"Yes, he did," said Pip. "We all knew your mama. Very well."

The answer surprised him. In the shadowy hallway House blinked back tears. Everyone knew his mama but him. But of course they would have known her.

"Your mama was special," Pip said.

Hearing his mother was special to someone else was more than House was ready for. "I'm sorry," he mumbled. His nose began to drip.

"Sorry by itself doesn't do anybody any good, son. You got to open your mind, House Jackson. You got to wonder. You got to open your heart." Pip aimed the flashlight beam at the library door. "You got business in there?"

House shoved his hands in his pockets and shook his head no.

"I think you do," said Pip. "Norwood said you'd be here the night he passed. He said to wait for you. Now I have." He handed House the flashlight. "'Lectric was canceled today—they cut off the juice." He walked to the front door, where his figure was an inky spot in the darkness. "I told you that baseball story for a reason, son. It's up to you to figure out the meaning of it. So I'll leave you to your business. Good night." He turned to go, hesitated, and then spoke one more time. He kept his back to House.

"I know you don't like my girl right now. I know she made it hard for you last year."

"Yessir."

"She didn't mean to."

And with that, Parting Schotz walked out the front door of Mr. Norwood Boyd's home and shut the door behind him, leaving House alone with only Eudora Welty and a hallway of old photographs for company.

★ 15 ★

Produce great Persons, the rest follows.

—Walt Whitman

House shone his light on the photograph of Pip in the baseball uniform. He could see the resemblance to Pip the old man. It was in the eyes, in the smile. *Aurora Angels.* "How about that?" he whispered.

The Aurora County All-Stars weren't organized, they had no uniforms, and they played only one official game a season, but it didn't matter what color you were—if you were a boy living in Aurora County and you loved the crack of the bat or the feel of the ball, or the sound of the wind in your ears as you ran the bases, you could play ball.

He stared at all the photographs. Maybe he was looking right at his mother, somewhere on this wall. What would she have looked like as a girl? Norwood Boyd was so much older than his mother would have been. How did she know him? Questions. He had questions.

He opened the tall door to the library and stepped in, the flashlight beam lighting his way. It was an enormous room with high windows facing the front of the house and a long sofa in the middle of the room, facing the far wall. The walls were lined, floor to ceiling, with books. In the past year House had read seventeen books to Norwood Boyd, all of them from this library. Every afternoon when House arrived, he'd pick up the current book from the nightstand, open it to the ribboned bookmark that saved their place, and Mr. Norwood would sigh. "Let's see what Long John Silver is up to today," he might say. He would smile when he said it. Then he would settle in and be silent, and House would read for almost an hour, until Mr. Norwood Boyd fell asleep. Then he was free to go. Sometimes Pip would arrive when he was reading. Sometimes it would be Miss Mattie. Someone would take his place, and he would go home with the latest chapter of a story in his head. He had begun to look forward to the next chapters as much as Mr. Norwood did. He and Norwood Boyd had shared an unspoken camaraderie in those late-afternoon hours.

House counted bookcases until he came to the fifth bookcase to the right of the door. He stood on a step stool to reach the seventh shelf. He shone the flashlight across the row of old books until he came to the only green spine. He pulled the book off the shelf and saw that it had fancy scrollwork on the cover. He climbed off the step stool before he would allow himself to read the title by flashlight: *Leaves of Grass* by Walt Whitman. It looked familiar, but he couldn't place where he might have seen it before.

He fished the note out of his pocket and reread the words Mr. Norwood Boyd wrote:

After the dazzle of day is gone,
Only the dark, dark night shows to my eyes the stars.
After the clangor of organ majestic, or chorus, or perfect band,
Silent, athwart my soul, moves the symphony true.
—Walt Whitman, Leaves of Grass

Your mother gave these words to me;
Now I give them to you as treasure for the days ahead.
Look for me in every atom that you see.

House opened the book and looked at the inside front cover. Written in a beautiful, careful script were the words *Elizabeth Jackson.* House stared at the signature until he couldn't see it anymore. He rubbed his eyes with weariness. It didn't make sense. "Symphony true," his mother had said in his dream. She had sung the song to House when he was little. *Moves the symphony true.* "Listen for that symphony, House," she had said.

He listened. He heard nothing.

And what should he do now?

He considered the situation. An old pug-dog slept next to House in Mr. Norwood Boyd's library. An old man had told House a story about baseball that was supposed to mean something—but what? Another old man had died and left House a treasure—a symphony true. And his mother...how did she figure in?

A mockingbird sang an insistent song in a tree outside the library windows. House had a half-mile walk back home. And, as he got to his feet clutching his incomprehensible treasure, he realized something: It would soon be exactly twenty-four hours to the minute since he had come to Mr. Norwood Boyd's ghostly home in the almost light of yesterday, when he had been awakened by Eudora Welty. He had followed the dog back to Mr. Norwood Boyd's and had found the man almost dead.

He had followed the instructions his father had given him many times, to call Doc MacRee if there was ever a problem. And he had taken one last look at Mr. Norwood Boyd. There had been a book at the end of his bed. He'd made note of it when he came into the bedroom but had forgotten about it until now. It had been green with fancy scrollwork on the cover. It was the same book he was now holding. *Leaves of Grass.* A long shiver grabbed House by the shoulders.

He looked at the book, and he looked at Eudora. Had she been wearing the note in her collar when she first came to get him? He couldn't remember. He only remembered seeing it when he crouched inside the honeysuckle bush. So how did Eudora get the note in her collar?

Like an answer to his question, a body rose from the couch.

★ 16 ★

I hated to bat against Drysdale. After he hit you he'd come around, look at the bruise on your arm and say, "Do you want me to sign it?"

—Mickey Mantle, center fielder, New York Yankees

House dropped the book and the flashlight; they clattered to the floor like tiny firecrackers exploding in a shower of light. Eudora yelped and plastered herself to the rug. House tried to run but his legs were rubber. He willed his heart to keep beating.

Bathed in the moonlight coming through the tall front windows, the body rising from the couch was no more than a soft shadow. And its voice, it turned out, was a whisper. "House?"

Cleebo! The blood rushed back to House's head along with his breath. In two seconds he was on top of Cleebo, throttling him like he was wrestling a chicken to the ground to cut off its head. "You!"

Cleebo's body went soft like a floppy doll but still House couldn't stop pummeling his friend. Cleebo began to cry. "I thought you was a ghost!"

House shook Cleebo by the shoulders and shouted at him. "What are you doing here?"

Cleebo cried harder. "Stop it, House!"

House released his friend and Cleebo mopped at his face. "I told my mama I was spendin' the night with you," he sobbed. "I snuck in here . . . hours ago! . . . got scared . . . climbed up in this old couch . . . musta fell asleep! Next thing I know I hear . . . I hear . . ." Cleebo hiccuped a huge breath and kept going. ". . . something in this room—I knew it was a ghost—I knew it—I was a goner, for sure!"

House shoved Cleebo back into the couch. "You sleep like the dead, Cleebo," he said. He tried to keep the shake out of his voice. "I've been here for ages!"

Cleebo wiped at his eyes while he cried some more. "All I wanted was to find the treasure—just like you!"

"There ain't no treasure, Cleebo!"

Cleebo's face wore the look of a little boy who'd just been told there were no more ice pops in the freezer. "You already looked?"

House didn't hesitate. "No! Yes!"

Cleebo sniffed through his tears and tried to stop crying. He wiped his nose with his T-shirt. "You ain't gonna tell nobody I cried, are you?"

House's anger fizzled as his fear dissolved. The room was quiet again. He watched a spider skittle away from the cone of yellow light on the floor. Eudora Welty trembled next to the couch.

"Swear you won't tell." Cleebo scrambled to his feet in the soft dark and stepped in place, side to side, toe to toe, hugging himself.

House picked up the flashlight and played it across the floor until he found *Leaves of Grass.* He picked it up with one hand while he gave Eudora a slow stroke with the other. The dog snuffled a sigh and closed her eyes.

"I'm dyin' here, House!" said Cleebo. "Swear you won't tell!"

House slumped into an armchair and settled into it like he was an old bag of beans filling in all the crevices. He switched off the flashlight. The room lost any yellow light it had possessed; the far walls of books shimmered in a dim silvery glow from beyond the windows where the world was stretching out in the darkness to nowhere, never ending.

"Be still!" House commanded. Cleebo stood as still as a stick.

House's insides were full to bursting. He'd held his secrets inside for such a long time. He looked at Cleebo's desperate face and made a decision. "I'll tell you somethin' I won't tell anybody else," he said, "and if you don't tell, I won't tell anybody about you crying."

Cleebo sank back on the couch with a grateful thump. "Done," he said wearily, relief spreading over him like soft butter on hot toast. "It's a deal."

And so, enveloped in the light from the morning moon, House unburdened himself to his friend. He told him what he'd been doing every afternoon for almost a year. He told him everything but the story of finding Mr. Norwood Boyd on his deathbed. He hadn't been able to tell his father about it, and now he found he couldn't tell Cleebo, either. The very act of dying was so precious, so private. And, truth to tell, a part of House wondered if he had somehow been summoned to keep watch with Norwood Boyd as the angels came to take him to heaven, in the same way that he'd watched the angels come for his mother, six years ago. Surely, those who were summoned to attend the dying were charged with holding that moment sacred. He would keep it to himself. He would keep his note to himself as well. But everything else, the whole year of coming and coming to Mr. Norwood Boyd's house and of reading and reading book after book, he shared this story.

"Why didn't you tell me you were coming over here every day? I coulda come with you!" Cleebo wore his disappointment like his wrinkled clothes, slopping all over the place.

"I didn't tell anybody, Cleebo!"

"But I'm your best friend!"

"I didn't even think to ask!"

"What did he look like?"

"He was old and wrinkled, like Pip."

"Was he always in bed?"

"When I got here he was."

"Did he talk?"

"Sure he talked."

"What did he say?"

"Not a lot. 'How are you, House? Thanks for coming, House . . .'" He stopped himself as he remembered.

"What?"

House bit his lip.

"What was the last thing he said to you?"

House heard it. The morning that he had been summoned by Eudora Welty, the last time he had sat next to the rosewood bed, Mr. Norwood had closed his eyes and spoken his last words on this earth: *I have enjoyed your company, House.*

House swallowed around a lump in his throat. "I don't remember."

"Can I see his room? Can I see where he died?"

"No!"

"Did you check the freezer for babies?"

"Stop it! I read seventeen books cover to cover while you were having fun catching pop flies and running the bases. And I can tell you: Mr. Norwood Boyd isn't a circus sideshow, he's a person. Or . . . he was."

"Why did he shut himself up in this house all these years?"

"I don't know. I didn't ask him."

"The guys ain't never gonna believe you did this..."

"You ain't gonna tell 'em!"

"Oh. Right." Cleebo scratched his head. "Why not?"

"They believe those stories about babies and ghosts and killings. And they'll call me as crazy as they called Norwood Boyd."

"Well, I feel sorry for you," said Cleebo. "Why would your daddy want to punish you like that? You couldn't play ball, but you could have come and watched."

House shook his head. "Watching's like torture when you can't play. And besides, Mr. Norwood..." House hesitated.

"What?"

House's face flushed. "He was a friend of the family."

Cleebo's eyes bugged wide. "How so!"

"I don't know." House was not willing to go further. "That's what my dad said."

"Wonder what's his connection to Frances."

"I can tell you that," said House. "If you're brave enough to walk into that hallway."

I think of few heroic actions which cannot be traced to the artistical impulse. He who does great deeds, does them from his innate sensitiveness to moral beauty.

—Walt Whitman

The flashlight made a puddle of light bobbling on the pictures in the hallway.

"Pip's like Jackie Robinson!" whispered Cleebo after House told him the story. "Did he play second base like Jackie?"

"I don't know... I didn't ask him," said House.

"And Mean-Man—just like Pee Wee Reese!"

House shook his head. "Pee Wee was a shortstop. Mr. Norwood was a catcher."

Cleebo shook his head. "That's not what I'm talkin' about. Nineteen forty-seven Brooklyn Dodgers. First season a black man played in the major leagues. There were folks in the stands—even in the dugouts!—who screamed at Jackie to go back to Africa—and worse—when he came onto the field to play. They screamed at Jackie Robinson! Jackie Robinson, who made six All-Star teams in a row! Jackie Robinson, who was National League MVP in 1949! And nobody has stole more bases than Jackie Robinson!"

"What about Pee Wee?"

"Oh. In the middle of all that screaming, Pee Wee Reese walked across the infield and clapped his white hand on Jackie Robinson's black shoulder. Pee Wee said, *This man is my teammate.* And everybody got quiet. And then they played ball."

House blinked. "How'd you know that?"

"You know my daddy—I've heard that story around my dinner table for years. Jackie stood tall, and Pee Wee stood with him. You don't know that story?"

House shook his head. "I know Sandy Koufax made 382 strikeouts in 1965. That's one less than Nolan Ryan's 383, and he did it when Nolan Ryan was still pitching in high school. Did you know that story?"

"You only told me a million times." Cleebo's eyes traveled the wall of photographs. "I wish I coulda seen Jackie Robinson steal home plate," he said in a faraway voice. He took the flashlight from House and leaned in close to Pip's picture. "Who woulda guessed Pip played ball?" His voice had a new respect in it. "And just look at that uniform. Aurora Angels..."

"Yeah," said House. "And Little League, like the kids in Jones County."

"Little League," sighed Cleebo. "You know, we'd have enough boys if we could pull 'em from all these little crossroads around here."

For a moment, both boys gazed at the photograph in silence. Then Cleebo shook his head. "We just *got* to play our game on July Fourth, House. Can't you figure somethin' out? The Mamas have all gone crazy. My mama tells me I'm going to be the next Sidney Poitier—who the heck is that? It ain't so, House. Ain't none of us boys gonna go to Hollywood."

"I know," said House. "I know." His mind ticked around the problem. "I want to play, too. I want to play real bad. But I don't know what to do about it." He gave a short whistle for Eudora, who snuffled out to the hallway, her tongue drooping out of her mouth. "Let's go, girl."

"We got to figure out somethin'," said Cleebo.

As they shut the big front door behind them, House said, "Don't tell me I don't *approach* stuff."

"Well, you sure got a whopper to tell now," said Cleebo.

"You promised you wouldn't tell."

"I won't. You don't tell on me, neither."

"You can count on me," said House.

The trio—House, Cleebo, and Eudora Welty—walked through the woodsy night to House's house. They walked through the same woods House had come through the morning that Norwood Boyd had died. A hundred years had passed since then. A chickadee called up the sun. It wouldn't be long before dawn.

"I can't believe Frances is related to Pip," said Cleebo. "Pip's amazing."

"You didn't think he was amazing before."

"That's before I knew he was like Jackie Robinson!"

"Pip says Mr. Norwood was amazing."

"Hmph!" said Cleebo. Overhead, an owl hooted his good night. "What's that book?"

House clutched his treasure closer to himself. "Just an old book."

"Oh, yeah? What's it about?"

"Nuthin' much."

Cleebo raised an eyebrow. "We got practice in the mornin', you know."

"I know."

"We gotta work on your knuckleball."

"We gotta sleep."

Leonard Jackson's light was off, but the back porch light shone into the morning dew. House had not turned it on when he left. Quietly the boys and Eudora tiptoed to bed on the sleeping porch. House tucked his note from Mr. Norwood Boyd inside his treasure and put it under his pillow.

Cleebo slept on the far side of the same big bed. He

snored louder than Eudora. Together they made a snoring symphony. *A symphony true,* thought House. As he fell asleep it came to him that maybe things happened, maybe people came into your life and went out again in their own way, in their own time, in concert with everything else. Maybe his mother would tell him about Mr. Norwood Boyd if he could find her again, in his dreams.

The night became day once again. It would be another hot one. It would be hotter than House ever could have imagined.

WBAC

IN BEAUTIFUL AURORA COUNTY

YOUR STATION FOR LOCAL NEWS AND WEATHER!

RADIO FLASH NEWS!

Composed and Read by Phoebe "Scoop" Tolbert

June 18, 6am

The Sunshine Laundry in Halleluia has become the *community gathering place in Our Fair County! The enormous plate-glass windows in front invite customers in to sit at the red-checkered tables and watch* Each Life Daily Turns *on the big television set mounted on the wall while they wait for their sheets and shirts to be ironed by Lurleen Wallace, who has almost mastered the pressing machine.*

I took my microphone to the street yesterday and became your on-the-scene reporter in the front room of the Sunshine Laundry at lunchtime. Here is just some of what I recorded:

Mary Wilson: *I hope to be the official laundry of the Aurora County Birthday Pageant!*

Woodrow "Pete" Wilson: *I protest this pageant—what about the ball game? My boy Cleebo needs to play in his game!*

Mary Wilson: *Shush, Pete! We've discussed this! His Hollywood career is more important!*

Every Mama Present: *That's right! This is a once-in-a-lifetime opportunity!*

Betty Ramsey: *Shhhh! The commercial's over! There he is, Dr. Dan! Coming to our town soon!*

Pip Schotz: *Can't be soon enough—that boy hasn't been home in five years. Are my shaving towels ready, Mary?*

Evelyn Lavender: *Are you starching* everything, *Mary?*

Mattie Perkins: *Phoebe, will you turn that thing off!*

Oops! Strike that last one!

As you can see, excitement is building for the Aurora County Birthday Pageant, in spite of some dissension in the ranks, which is always the case when one is creating art! This reporter can't wait to find out how the matter is resolved, as my grandsons still will not eat their vegetables, and soon we are going to have to break out the castor oil. Please, let us resolve this issue. We need to address my grandsons' digestion if nothing else!

★ 18 ★

Trying to throw a fastball by Hank Aaron is like trying to sneak the sun past a rooster.

—CURT SIMMONS, PITCHER, PHILADELPHIA PHILLIES

Cleebo snored through the night, but House slept fitfully. When he got out of bed he was starving—he hadn't eaten since breakfast the day before. He slipped *Leaves of Grass* out from under his pillow and padded into the kitchen while Cleebo and Honey were still sleeping. His father was already at work in the shed. He'd left a plate of fried bacon on a plate by the stove. House ate three bowls of cereal and pored over his treasure in the early morning sunlight.

Poetry. *Leaves of Grass* was poetry. The stories he'd read to Mr. Norwood Boyd—he'd understood them. He'd even admit that he liked them! But these poems . . . he wasn't sure what he was reading. He stared at his mother's handwriting again—*Elizabeth Jackson*—and at Mr. Norwood's note about the symphony song: *Your mother gave these words to me; Now I give them to you as treasure for the days ahead. Look for me in every atom that you see.*

The All-Stars needed rescuing in the days ahead. He stared at his note as if it held some magical answer. Finding a way to pitch in this ball game was his dilemma. The pageant was his cross to bear. And the symphony true... well, that was his mystery. Perhaps Mr. Norwood meant for the treasure to be used on this day—this very day. Their chance of playing was coming down to the wire and House was willing to grasp at any straw.

Cleebo jazzed into the kitchen searching for breakfast.

"Out of all the books you could get from Mean-Man, you got a book of poems!" he marveled. "What about adventure stories? Pirates? Killers? Rocket ships? Instead you got the-cat-sat-on-the-mat!"

"It's not like that," said House.

"Read me one." Cleebo reached for the mashed potato bowl.

"They're too long."

"Well, read a snippet, then." Cleebo emptied the cereal into the mashed potato bowl and poured on the milk.

House opened the book at random and found some lines underlined in blue ink:

"I CELEBRATE myself, and sing myself,
And what I assume you shall assume,
For every atom belonging to me as good belongs to you."

"That don't make sense," said Cleebo, crumbs spilling from his mouth, milk dribbling down his chin.

House closed the book. *Look for me in every atom that you see.* Was it too far-fetched to think that Mr. Norwood Boyd knew about House's dilemma, that he meant to help, even from beyond the grave? Nah. House was sunk and he knew it. He wouldn't get to pitch against the Redbugs at all. Just in case, though, he shoved the book into his backpack with his water and lunch and brought it with him to practice.

"Slide! Slide! Slide!" Ned Tolbert screamed.

Cleebo streaked from home to first. He hurled himself forward and reached for the bag. His body scraped the dirt and raised a tornado of dust as he slammed into first base, where Wilkie Collins caught the throw from Evan Evans and tagged Cleebo squarely on the bean.

"Safe!" hollered Ned's twin brother, Boon, who was playing catcher.

"He's out!" screamed Wilkie. He hoisted the ball heavenward and crow-hopped around the base like he was on fire.

"You're blind, Wilkie!" yelled Cleebo, dusting himself off and swelling with pride. "I was safe by a country mile!"

"Good play at first, and good catch, Wilkie!" shouted House from the pitcher's mound. "But Cleebo got there first—he's safe."

"Now watch me steal second!" gloated Cleebo. "I'm on a roll! Just like Jackie Robinson!" His clothes were coated with grit.

House shook his head. "You don't slide into first, how many times do I have to tell you?"

"He likes to slide," said Ned. "It gives his mama more laundry to do."

Cleebo swiped at Ned, but Ned bobbed out of the way.

"You gotta catch now, Cleebo," said House. "We don't have enough players to let you run the bases, and I need Boon in the outfield—Ned's a power hitter."

"Aw, House!"

"I need a catcher!"

"Come on, Cleebo!" shouted Ned, on deck, swinging his Wonderboy! bat at the air. "I'm up!"

"I'm always the one to sacrifice!" yelled Cleebo. "I want a run at the bases before we're through!"

"Deal," said House. "But we only got a little while before—"

"Don't remind me!" shouted Cleebo. His voice gurgled with frustration. "I know what's comin'."

They all did. Pageant practice was scheduled for 9:00 A.M. Desperation had brought the ballplayers to the field at 8:00. House's head had been full of clangor and questions at the kitchen table, but now that he was standing on the pitcher's mound, his focus was crystal clear.

He shook out both arms to get ready for his windup. When Koufax pitched, his back leg was tethered to the mound, but the rest of him was flying, every muscle moving in a kind of lightning-fast ballet. Cleebo hunkered down behind the plate. He smacked his fist into his glove. "Just lob it over to start with, House, don't try no pyrotechnics."

House leaned back into the stance, came forward in one long, fluid motion like Koufax, and brought his arm completely overhand and stretched forward with a fastball throw.

"Wide!" said Cleebo. He threw the ball back to House.

House reared back and zinged a hard fastball to Cleebo, inside and high. Cleebo stretched and snagged it.

"Try again," he said. "Not so hard!"

"Let's have a batter!" shouted House.

Ned stepped into the batter's box and swung through. "Shoot me that knuckleball, House! I'm ready!"

"Step out of the box, Ned," ordered Cleebo. He got down to business. "House! Don't pull so far back in your windup. I don't care what Koufax did, you can't see the strike zone when you're that far back—your arm's in the way, and that's why the ball is going wild."

House nodded. Not so far back. Still, a high-kicking

windup, long forward movement toward the plate. A curveball, spun with the middle finger, curved vertically from the overhand throw. Just like Koufax.

"Better," said Cleebo, catching it handily and tossing it back to House. "Try your fastball."

House gripped the ball with his fingers across the wide part of the seam, wound up, and threw again. And again. And one more time.

"C'mon," cried the outfield. "Let's see some action!"

His arm was fine. Better than fine. He was sure he could feel twinges of pain from his shoulder to his elbow. But if Koufax could do it, so could he.

He struck out Ned. Cleebo threw the ball to third base and the infielders threw around the horn. "You gotta let 'em hit the ball, House," said Cleebo, "or we won't none of us get any practice! You don't have to throw so hard."

House obliged. Everybody hit. Lincoln Latham picked up a bad hop at second. Ned caught every pop fly. Boon got some lumber on the ball and hit a long line drive toward third. Evan Evans caught it at his gut, stumbled backward, and still gathered enough forward motion to toss the ball to House, who had run to second base. House and Evan began a pickle play with Arnold Hindman, the runner, between them. Shouts played all around the field as Arnold ran back and forth between second and third, with House and Evan closing the gap and tossing the ball from one to the other in the rundown, until Evan finally tagged Arnold out.

"You gotta learn to slide, Arnie!" yelled Cleebo, who had run to cover third.

Boon had tagged first, where he stood on the bag, next to Wilkie, and shouted, "You coulda thrown it to first and got me out!"

"The play was at third," said House. "Besides, Wilkie can't catch from that far away."

"I should be playing first base," said Cleebo.

"Well, I can't play catcher!" said Wilkie.

"That's for sure!" said Cleebo.

"I can!" Striding toward the mound with her catcher's mitt on her left hand came Ruby Lavender.

We convince by our presence.

—Walt Whitman

"Not you!" said Cleebo. He sprinted back to home plate and almost splayed himself over it. "This is my plate! I say who catches here!"

"Really?" Ruby looked at House, who adjusted his baseball cap and sighed.

"She's a girl!" yelled Ned.

"You're brilliant, Ned!" hollered Boon from left field.

"Don't forget our bylaws!" cried Evan Evans from third.

"That's right!" said Cleebo with great satisfaction. "No girls. And especially since you-know-what!"

Ruby pulled up her left overalls strap. "Cleebo, you've played ball with me ever since I can remember!" She pointed at Boon and Ned. "And so have you! Right in my back meadow! With my grandma! And your daddy, too, Cleebo. And now you're going to tell me that I'm not good enough because you're all mad at Frances for breaking House's arm, so now no girls can play? That's just plain stupid."

"How so?" Cleebo stuck out his chin.

"If you'd let girls play you'd have enough players for a full team. You want to play so much, you should be happy you've got another player, Cleebo—I'm just as good a catcher as you are, and you know it!"

"She *is* pretty good," said Boon.

"Do girls play on Little League teams in Jones County?" asked Ned.

"I don't know," said House.

"You'd better believe they do!" said Ruby. "You boys aren't thinking straight."

"Well, we never had to think about it before you showed up wanting to play," said Ned.

House's mind bubbled back to the thoughts he'd had in the kitchen. Maybe a rescue was possible after all. He pointed at Cleebo. "You want to have a run at the bases?"

"You know I do."

"Grab a bat," said House. "Ruby, you catch."

Ruby grabbed a ball from the bucket by the backstop.

"Hey!" yelled Evan and Lincoln and Arnold.

"Wait a minute!" Cleebo stood his ground over home

plate. "You tricked me! I ain't playing ball with no girl! Next thing you know, we'll all have our arms broken!"

Before the arguing could escalate, Leonard Jackson's truck came dusting down the dirt road near the ball field. In the back was a giant silver pressing machine from the Sunshine Laundry. Waving both arms from the open window at the passenger seat and hollering herself blue in the face was Mary Wilson.

"Cleebo Wilson, you git yourself over to pageant practice this instant! I've got to get this machine repaired and I can't be worrying about your whereabouts! I got laundry piled to the skies waiting for pressing! Git now! Git!"

"Ha, Cleebo! You gotta git!" said Boon.

"And the rest of you! Git!" said Mary Wilson. She pointed to the chinaberry tree behind Halleluia School. "They're over there waiting on you! Shame on you boys! Get over there this minute!"

Each boy ducked his head in order to look suitably shamed. "Yes'm," they all said, including Ruby.

The truck came to a complete stop and dust swirled all around it in a little brown cloud. Leonard Jackson opened the back door of the cab and Honey slipped out of the truck with Eudora Welty, whom she had on a rope leash threaded through a white tutu. The sun washed the ball field in a brilliant, buttery glow that spread across home plate. Even the dust looked golden.

Leonard Jackson kissed his daughter good-bye, waved

at House and the boys, and called, "I'll be back later—we've got a big breakdown here to tend to."

"Yessir," said House.

"You've got Honey's lunch?"

"In my backpack."

"See you soon—"

"Git!" yelled Mary Wilson. Leonard Jackson shrugged at the boys. Some of them shrugged back. The truck rolled on toward Jackson's Mowing and Small Engine Repair.

Cleebo scratched at his forehead. "I don't know what's worse," he said in a defeated voice. "Too much starch or too many Mamas."

"Your mama is the Queen Poo-bah of the Mamas," said Boon. "We can't ignore her." The boys looked across the field at the little band of kids gathered under the chinaberry tree like little bobbing corks on a dusty brown lake. They were moving together, doing some sort of dance, or play, or . . . something.

"We're on death row," said Wilkie. "There's no getting out of this."

"Heads up!" called Ruby. She threw her baseball hard to House, who stretched his arm out and caught it almost automatically. Nobody said a word.

And slowly, walking like they were heading to their own hangings, the boys and Ruby made their way to the chinaberry tree. A happy Honey led the way, as if she was a drum majorette, high-stepping her way to her destiny, with Eudora Welty panting and trotting at her side.

House picked up his backpack by the backstop and brought up the rear, walking across the weedy field by himself. There would be no rescue, not from Norwood Boyd, not from his mother, not from anybody. There was no magic, there was no mystery, there was no symphony. There were just these facts: There would be no game. He would not pitch. His career was over before it began. He struggled not to cry.

★ 20 ★

If you come to a fork in the road, take it.

—Yogi Berra, catcher, New York Yankees

"The *show must go on, mes amis!*" Finesse dabbed her eyes with a Snowberger's handkerchief—a huge handkerchief embroidered with a giant *S* that Snowberger's Funeral Home had been giving out to the bereaved for years. Now Finesse owned one, and she used it to good effect. The handkerchief was white. Everything else about Finesse was black. All black. Even her lipstick was black. She spoke through the mesh of a black veil. She wore no jewelry—she was in mourning, after all—but three enormous black feathers protruded from her hat. *She's a big, black horned toad,* thought House.

"She looks like a black widow spider!" said Ruby.

"... who caught a vulture!" said George.

Melba stood next to Finesse, clutching her clipboard and hissing like a death-row warden. "Shhhh!"

Finesse held up a black-gloved hand as if she were signaling leniency for the doomed. "I am glad to see you all this morning, even though many of you are late—very late! I had every confidence you would join us, however. We have already divined some dances and skits—rest assured, we will fit you in. But let me begin at the beginning, now that I have you all assembled!"

Finesse cleared her throat. "As you all know," she said, "I was forced to leave you abruptly yesterday. One of our eldest citizens, Mr. Norwood Rhinehart Beauregard Boyd, has..." Finesse put her handkerchief to her mouth for a long moment and then sputtered melodramatically, "... died! He's *dead, mes amis,* dead as a doornail, I saw it with my own two eyes, my great-granddaddy's greatest boyhood friend, laying out at Snowberger's, still as... death!" She sobbed one great sob into her handkerchief.

House and Cleebo exchanged a look.

Ruby blinked in amazement. "Pip was Mr. Norwood's boyhood friend?"

"I didn't know he had any friends, ever!" said Wilkie Collins.

"Of course he had friends!" said Finesse.

"Are you sure he's dead?" asked Cleebo.

"He's as dead as beautiful, young Emily Webb in *Our Town* by Thornton Wilder!" choked Finesse. She blew her nose in a ladylike manner. "Mr. Norwood Boyd asked for no funeral, no memorial service," she said, dabbing at her eyes. "But...but..." Finesse struggled to compose herself. She took a deep breath. "I think we are meant somehow to honor him with our pageant."

House blinked.

"Mean-Man Boyd?" said Evan Evans. "What are we supposed to do—kidnap kids around the county?"

"Cook 'em?" said Arnold Hindman. Hesitant laughter rolled around the ballplayers. House kept silent. Finesse looked stricken.

"None of these exaggerations is true, *mes amis,*" she said, fresh tears in her eyes. "These are rumors, lies! Mr. Norwood Boyd was a great man! My great-granddaddy can tell you the truth—doesn't anyone here know the truth about Mr. Norwood Boyd?"

House felt a prick at the back of his conscience. Still, he kept his thoughts to himself.

"Ghosts!" cried Honey. She hugged Eudora Welty.

"I know somethin' about him!" shouted Cleebo. He caught himself as House sucked in his breath and glared at Cleebo.

"What do you know?" Finesse was suddenly delighted. "Do tell!"

Cleebo glanced at House and changed his mind. "I know you ain't even related to the man, that's what I know!"

Finesse straightened her shoulders. "Related is a relative term, *mon ami.* And I know something, too, Cleebo Wilson." She pulled a piece of paper from her straw tote bag and opened it carefully. "My great-granddaddy was left a note by Mr. Norwood Boyd."

The blood evaporated from House's face. A tingle spread across his shoulders.

"I wanted to keep it private," Finesse said, "but Poppy told me I must share it with you all because... because it has meaning for our town on its birthday, and because our most famous citizen, Dr. Dan Deavers, who ordered this pageant in the first place, would certainly approve... so I shall read it."

Finesse took a deep breath. So did House.

"This note is shrouded in mystery, *mes amis,*" said Finesse, "*enveloppe de mystère!*" Finesse pointed a black-gloved finger at House. "One must not read too much into such mystery..."

"Read the dang note!" growled Cleebo. Finesse cleared her throat, snapped the note in front of her flamboyantly, and read:

"I see great things in baseball. It will take our people out-of-doors, fill them with

oxygen, give them a larger physical stoicism, tend to relieve us from being a nervous, dyspeptic set, repair those losses and be a blessing to us."

—Walt Whitman

Whitman! Baseball! House rocketed upright. He was dizzy with the thought.

Cleebo scrambled to his feet. "That's what I say! *Dispepper* and all! A blessing! Baseball!" He sliced his glove back and forth in Finesse's direction, as if he might decapitate her with it. "Look. Me and some of the team were discussing it on the way over here and we decided we ain't gonna participate in no pageant! We need to play our game!"

"I'm playing!" shouted Ruby.

"No, you ain't," said Cleebo. "House!"

But House's mind was somewhere else. In the midst of the clangor, he began to ask questions. Why would Frances have a note from Mr. Norwood Boyd? A note about baseball?

Kids were talking all at once, like... like an organ majestic. A perfect band.

And *baseball*. What about baseball? House began pacing. Mr. Norwood Boyd was trying to tell him something, he was sure of it.

Melba Jane stomped a sandaled foot and shouted, "Come to order! Hush right this minute!"

"Oh, go stuff it, Melba Jane!" hollered Cleebo. "We don't have to pay attention to you!"

Honey tiptoed Eudora away from the crowd and plopped down with her by the hose. She put her hands over Eudora's ears and watched.

"Cleebo!" cried Melba with indignation. "Dr. Dan Deavers is coming to this pageant and your mama..."

"My mama nuthin'!" said Cleebo. "This is stupid! I'm gonna get my dad out here..."

"Lots of luck!" said Boon.

Finesse put her hands in front of her in a praying pose, bent her head, and stood silently until the group calmed. She looked up when all was quiet and said, "It seems we have a revolt."

Before anyone could agree with her, House said in a clear voice, "No, we don't." He gestured to the ball team. "We'll be in the pageant." He had no idea what it meant—just that it was true.

"You will?" said Finesse.

"We will?" said the ballplayers.

"No we won't!" said Cleebo.

But House had figured out something—*moves the symphony true.* He knew what it meant. "We can do what we want, right?" he asked Finesse. "You said it's *our pageant...*"

"Yes...," said Finesse in an uncertain voice.

"Then, we'll play baseball," said House. "And we'll have a pageant."

"How do we do that?" Finesse had her handkerchief at her throat.

"I don't know," said House. "You're the artistic genius, you figure it out."

His face was hot with embarrassment, but there was a rightness to the words, so he kept on going in spite of himself. He tried not to think about the fact that he was talking more than he'd ever talked in front of people in his entire life, and that he was actually suggesting cooperating with his toad, Frances Schotz, making a spectacle out of himself and everyone else.

He let his soul speak. Or maybe it was the voice of Mr. Norwood Boyd's ghostly spirit, or the influence of Pip's sad story. Maybe it was those words from Walt Whitman, written so long ago, the same words his mother had loved and sung. Suddenly it was all connected. Suddenly it made sense. Suddenly he had words to say:

"*Anybody* who wants to play ball can play."

Kids scrambled to their feet, excited.

Ruby hugged herself. "Yes!"

"No!" shouted Finesse and Melba and Cleebo all at the same time.

"Yes!" said House and Ruby together.

House entreated his ballplayers—"Your mamas want you in this pageant," he said. "And you want to play ball—

we can do both! Everybody wins. We'll beat them Redbugs—you'll see."

"I don't want to play ball!" shouted Honey. "I want to tap-dance!"

House scooped his sister into his arms. "You can be a dancer, Honey."

It came together for House, the mystery, the symphony, and he knew what he had to do. It involved dazzle and clangor, chorus majestic and perfect band. It included Frances Schotz and Ruby and Melba and Cleebo and Honey and Miss Mattie, his father, the ballplayers, the Mamas, all of Aurora County, Mississippi, even Eudora Welty. It involved baseball. A pageant. Several tutus, most likely. And one beautiful treasure.

The one thing House didn't bargain on was the betrayal.

★ 21 ★

Have you heard that it was good to gain the day?
I also say it is good to fall, battles are lost
in the same spirit in which they are won.
—Walt Whitman

Finesse grabbed control as best she could. "You left us with half a pageant this morning when you didn't show up on time." She tugged on each gloved finger, removed her black gloves, and continued. "We did the best we could without you. We had to assign parts as we had a need for them. Some of you won't be happy with your assignments, but that's life—*C'est la vie!* We will need everyone's sizes—pants, shirts, leotards—as Miss Mary Wilson"—she pointed at Cleebo—"your mama! is going to help us with costumes and we want them to fit."

"They'll crackle when you move in 'em!" said Wilkie.

"Shut up, Blind Boy!" said Cleebo.

A gaggle of crows argued in the top of the chinaberry

tree. House tried to think fast. "Who's got paper and pen? Melba?"

Melba looked at Finesse for permission. Finesse gave a tiny shrug of approval. Melba handed House her clipboard and pencil.

House scribbled furiously. "Me and the team need some things."

"We need good sense," said Cleebo, "and a new captain."

"You're gonna play, Cleebo," said House.

"Yeah. Me and every fruitcake in the county! No way are we gonna win this game—you'll have so many kids turn out for this you won't know where to put them! You'll end up with Blind Boy Wilkie at umpire—"

"I ain't blind!" cried Wilkie. "I just got thick glasses!"

"—you'll let Ruby catch and you'll put that sorry excuse for a dog out there fielding foul balls!"

"I'm a better catcher than you'll ever be, Cleebo Wilson!" said Ruby.

"YouDoggie is not sorry!" Honey kissed the dog's wrinkled head. "Would you like some sandwich, YouDoggie? Let Mama see..." She opened House's backpack.

"Here's our list." House handed the clipboard to Finesse. "This is for all of us."

"Really, House..." Finesse perused the list. "Your penmanship, honestly!" But she read out loud the baseball team's requests:

baseball uniforms and caps
real bases and a real pitcher's mound
new bats
new baseballs
a catcher's mask and kneepads
a cooler with lots of ice water
one pair of tap shoes, size small

Honey clapped at the mention of tap shoes. "Want some more, YouDoggie?" Eudora Welty, wearing her white tutu, snorted next to Honey and snuffled at the last sandwich piece Honey had given her. "Good girl," said Honey. "In a minute I'll pour you some water." Eudora wagged her tail.

"These things cost money," said Finesse.

"I thought your uncle was giving us money."

"That's right," said Finesse, "for the pageant! Surely you don't expect us—all of us!—to actually *play* a game of baseball?" Finesse had lost her French. She was quickly losing her temper.

"It's the American game!" said House. "For an American town! On the American holiday—Fourth of July!" House opened his arms wide to include every kid. "We'll beat the pants off those Redbugs with all this talent."

Cleebo hooted. "Talent! You're blind, too!"

"We can certainly honor baseball," said Finesse, "we intend to. In fact, ever since I read that note from Mr.

Norwood Boyd, I was thinking about a baseball dance number for you boys . . ."

"We don't dance," said Cleebo flatly.

"Yes, we do," said House.

"You're crazy," said Cleebo.

"I dance!" said Honey in a bright voice. She rummaged in House's backpack for a water bottle.

"We all dance," said House. He thought he must be feverish—even his eyes were hot. He couldn't stop talking. "It's a symphony. A symphony true. We'll do it all at the same time." Kids looked at House as if he had turned green right before their eyes.

"And how do you propose we do that?" Finesse crossed her arms in front of her. Melba followed suit.

"House!" chirped Honey. "There's a book in your lunch!" She held up *Leaves of Grass.* She used both hands.

"Hey!" said Cleebo. "I know that book! Give it here!"

"Honey, put that back!" House lunged for the book.

"Aha!" Cleebo grabbed the book as if it were a wild throw, a fifty-five-footer bouncing up from home plate and into his mitt.

"You gonna *read* to us, House? You gonna read us some *po-et-ry*?"

"Give it back, Cleebo!"

"I know this book!" he crowed. "And I know where it come from!"

★ 22 ★

I became a good pitcher when I stopped trying to make them miss the ball and started trying to make them hit it.
—Sandy Koufax, pitcher, Los Angeles Dodgers

Cleebo held the book up like it was a Bible and he was a revival preacher. He hollered at the top of his voice.

"You gonna read us a *book,* House?" Several ballplayers guffawed along with Cleebo. Honey cowered against Eudora. Ruby crossed her arms in front of her overalls and watched.

Cleebo opened the book and turned in a slow circle, showing the open pages to the group. "It's a bunch of *po-et-ry*!" His voice was hoarse. "A book of *po-et-ry* from a dead man's house!" Cleebo froze like he was a freeze-tag statue, making his point.

Finesse was shocked into silence, as was everyone else under the chinaberry tree. A scrap of paper fluttered from the open pages and settled, like a feather, into the shade under the tree.

House's knees wobbled. A wind rose up and a hoot owl called, such an unusual sound in the bright of day. The sun baked the earth and House made himself breathe. "It's a book by Walt Whitman," he said quietly. "The same guy who wrote about baseball in your note from Mr. Norwood, Frances."

Finesse bit her lip.

"This book explains what I'm talking about," House said. He picked up the scrap of paper and licked his lips.

"Here's a piece of it." He called on his mother and he called on Mr. Norwood Boyd, he straightened his shoulders, and he took the plunge. And he read them the poem.

"After the dazzle of day is gone,
Only the dark, dark night shows to my eyes the stars.
After the clangor of organ majestic, or chorus, or
perfect band,
Silent, athwart my soul, moves the symphony true."

Finesse took a step backward, as if her knees had given out on her. Melba rushed to her side. "Are you all right?" Finesse waved her off.

"There ain't nothin' about no baseball game in there," said Cleebo, "nor no pageant. And we ain't got us a organ or a chorus or a band. We just got a crazy ball team captain. I vote for a new captain. Who's with me?"

"Don't you see?" said House. He understood the connection. Mr. Norwood Boyd's time was over. House's time was now. He stepped into that moment where the past and the present meet and became more than he had been.

"It doesn't matter," he said. "It doesn't matter if we have a game or a pageant or both, it really doesn't matter. And you know why? Because we're all gonna be as dead as doornails one day, as dead as Mr. Norwood Boyd, and then what?"

The sun beamed through a cloud. There *would* be a rescue. House would provide it himself. "There's this symphony," he said, his voice clipped and sure. "It's everybody working together, it's—"

"You don't make no sense!" shouted Cleebo.

House shoved one hand in Cleebo's face like a stop sign. He took his book back with the other. "I'm talking, Cleebo. I'm *approaching* the problem. Shut. Up."

"I ain't gonna shut up! You're a crazy person!"

"Where'd you get that book?" asked Lincoln Latham.

"I can tell you where he got it!" said Cleebo, on fire. "He stole it! He stole it from Mean-Man Boyd!"

Kids squealed and gasped. Cleebo gathered steam from the clangor. He poked his finger at every ballplayer under the chinaberry tree. "Ned! Boon! Evan! All-a-you! We've every one of us suffered because of House for a whole year now! We lost our game last year for the first time ever because House let his arm be broken by a girl. He still don't have his arm completely back, we got a game in two weeks, and now he wants to turn us into dancers! He wants us to cooperate with the girl who lost our game for us! Is that what you want? And worse than that..." Cleebo stabbed his finger at House.

"This boy has been goin' over to Mean-Man's haunted house every day since he broke his arm! He's been workin' in cahoots with Baby-Eater Boyd! Read him cookbooks! Helped him cook all them kidnapped kids he's had cut up in the freezer for years! He's been eatin' those babies hisself—that's what's wrong with him, I tell you true! He's brainwashed!"

Even the birds stopped singing. No one spoke or moved.

"And why did he keep his doings a secret?" Cleebo was a geyser, spouting whatever came into his head next. "He wanted the treasure! Everybody knows that house is full of treasure! Where is it?" Sweat poured down Cleebo's angry face. "Where is it, House?"

Twenty-one children and one old dog breathed in quiet anticipation under the chinaberry tree and waited to see what would happen next.

Keep your face always toward the sunshine,
and shadows will fall behind you.
—Walt Whitman

Honey began to cry. Ruby sat next to her and put her arm around her. Eudora snuffled her snout into Honey's lap. Melba fanned Finesse with her clipboard. Cleebo mopped at his face with his shirtsleeve. And House took center stage. Now that they all knew, he was not about to let this moment get away from him.

He shoved his note into his pocket and drew himself up to his full height. "Mr. Norwood Boyd was a friend of my . . . family. And Cleebo is right. I went over to his house every day after my arm was broken."

Cleebo nodded at everyone and puffed out his chest as if he were being proven right, but House ignored him and so did everyone else. "I was asked to do it. And I was scared. I knew all the stories. But it wasn't like that."

House scratched the side of his face, trying to buy time; he was short of breath. His heart felt like it had swelled into his throat.

Cleebo's chest deflated and he shrank. He grew smaller by the minute.

"He never ate anybody," continued House. "He liked being alone. He was sick. He wanted to hear the stories he had read when he was a boy, so I read them to him. *Treasure Island* was the one we were reading when he died."

House's heart had swollen so much he couldn't take in a breath. So he held up a hand and stopped to catch his breath. It took a full minute. No one—not even Cleebo—moved. When he could breathe again House said in a quiet voice, "If there was a treasure, it was his friends. Mr. Norwood had friends." House bit his lower lip and finished his thought. "I was one of them."

In the moment he spoke the words, House knew that Pip had been right. House had loved Mr. Norwood Boyd. He had loved a man he had hardly known, but somehow he had known him well. It was the oddest thing.

Melba was holding her pencil so tightly she broke it. The noise popped the air and broke the spell. Ruby blinked and wiped her hair out of her eyes. Finesse held her handkerchief to her mouth. For once her tears seemed real.

Cleebo kicked at a rock and kids began to breathe again. Honey sniffed. House turned to Finesse. "Mr. Norwood Boyd loved baseball. Used to be, not every boy in this county could play baseball. Ask your great-granddaddy about it. And put that in your history of Aurora County—your American history—Frances."

He was done. All those words.

★ 24 ★

There is always some kid who may be seeing me for the first or last time—I owe him my best.
—JOE DIMAGGIO, CENTER FIELDER, NEW YORK YANKEES

"I don't know you no more," said Cleebo. He spit into the dirt.

"Yes, you do," said House. He looked Cleebo square in the face. "I'm somebody who keeps his word." Cleebo sat down with a thump.

Finesse recovered quickly. She lifted her veil, dabbed at her eyes, and cleared her throat. "That's an inspiring speech, House Jackson," she said. "I'm sure that if we could play a real baseball game, we would."

"Well, I'm playing ball," announced Ruby, rising to her feet. She looked at House with admiration. A little breeze blew through the crowd.

"Me, too," said every other kid in the crowd, as everyone

stood up and faced Finesse. Melba Jane looked horrified and nauseous. House blinked at the mutiny happening in front of his eyes.

"What about our plans from this morning?" Finesse asked. "What about the Sawmill Samba we worked on? What about the Pine Lake Prance and the Silvery Moon Skit?"

But kids were solidly behind House. Cleebo had lost. So had Finesse. Defeat crossed her face, and when it did, House saw a glimmer of something sadder than sad underneath it, but Finesse pulled herself together. She inhaled deeply and arched an eyebrow.

"*Mes amis?* Must we vote, then?"

"Wait!" said House. Mamas or no Mamas, Finesse was about to vote herself out of a job. But Finesse would not wait.

"Must we vote on the ball game—*base-ball* outdoors on a buggy empty lot—or the lovely pageant indoors on the bright new stage?"

"I got an idea," said House, but Finesse had her own ideas. Don Quixote directed her Sancho Panza to take the vote.

"How many for the pageant?" asked Melba, pencil poised over the clipboard. Not a hand was raised.

"Listen!" said House, but Finesse would not listen.

Melba took a long breath and asked the defining question: "How many for the . . . game?"

Every hand shot into the air.

"Very well," said Finesse. Her lips trembled. *"Très bien!* I know when I have been defeated!" She held up the list that House had given her. "We have no budget for a ball game. We do not need this list."

Theatrically, Finesse tore House's list in half and let the pieces flutter to the ground around her.

House took off his cap, smoothed back his hair, and shoved the cap back on his head. His forehead glistened with sweat.

"Mes amis," said Finesse. "You could have had my expertise—you should have seen my contributions to theater at the Lanyard School last year! Oh, what a production we could have had! But I will not be a party to this mockery of our wonderful American pageant! If you all choose a *base-ball* game as your pageant, so be it! It will not include *moi*! And so, *mes amis,* I tender you my *adieu*!"

Finesse snatched off her feathered hat and veil. Her eyes were volcanic. She slapped the headgear at Melba, who bobbled the feathers and the veil along with her clipboard.

"Here are my last words, *mes amis,*" spit Finesse. "I quit! *Je quitte!"*

She stamped away just as House grabbed her arm.

"Wait!"

She flung his arm away from her. "Who do you think

you are, House Jackson? And why do you need to torture me?"

"What are you talking about?"

"I know you hate me!"

"I . . . do not!"

"Yes, you do—say it!"

"Say what? That you broke my elbow? Okay—you broke my elbow! In two places! Bad!"

Finesse wailed as if she were in a confessional. "I know I broke your arm! I know you couldn't play ball! I know you were upset . . ."

"Upset doesn't begin to cover it!"

". . . and now you've turned everyone against me!"

"You've done that yourself with your crazy ways, Frances! You dress like a gooney bird and you act like a nut!" He shocked his own self. He was a boy of few words who had become a fountain of verbosity.

"Nobody wants to be in your stupid pageant—it's a big joke! We're only here because we have to be! Why don't you go back to Jackson and your prestigious Lanyard School and leave us alone?"

Melba wore a look of shock on her face. Every single kid was transfixed.

Finesse's mascara began to streak down her face along with her tears. "I agree that Mr. Norwood Boyd was a great man," she said. She wiped her mascara to either side of her cheeks with her fingers. "And you're not. You don't have the faintest idea about what really matters." She addressed the rest of the crowd. "None of you do."

She stalked across the empty field toward Main Street. Melba raced after her, feathers bouncing against the dirt and stirring up dust.

★ 25 ★

I often and silently come where you are
that I may be with you.
—Walt Whitman

Finesse looked like a big black smudge retreating to town.

"Great speech," said Cleebo. "It's about time."

"Don't talk to me," said House. "You're no friend of mine."

"Fine," said Cleebo. He crossed his arms over his chest. "Don't expect me to play in your ball game, neither."

"I don't," said House. "We've got a catcher."

Ruby nodded. "Now what?"

"We'd all better pray that Cleebo's mama doesn't come back from gettin' that machine fixed too soon," said Wilkie.

"That's a fact," said Boon. "We're in real trouble now."

"I'll be back," said House. "Honey, stay here."

"I'll keep her," Ruby volunteered.

House ran after Finesse. He passed Melba Jane and reached Finesse as she neared the barber pole outside of Pip's shop on Main Street.

"Stop, already!" he shouted.

Finesse stopped but kept her back to House. Melba Jane caught up and plastered herself like a silent bug against the barbershop's plate-glass window where she wouldn't miss a word.

"I can tell you how to make this work!" said House.

"I'm not interested!" Finesse spun to face House. Her face was a river of running black mascara, and her eyes were swollen from crying.

"Girls at the Lanyard School tried to tell me how to make things work, too!" She hiccuped into her handkerchief.

"I was the best Emily Webb in the history of the Lanyard School's annual production of Thornton Wilder's *Our Town*—Miss DeBivort even said so! I got deep inside my character—I inhabited her! I knew her, inside and out! I understood what she meant when she said, 'Do any human beings ever realize life while they live it?—every, every minute?'" Finesse looked heavenward as she slipped into character for a moment. Then she hid her face in her hands and sobbed. "But the girls at the Lanyard School just laughed at me! They said I was ridiculous! They snickered behind my back all year! Do you know how that makes a person feel?"

"You bet I do!" said House. "You left town and I had to stay here and be laughed at. You know what the guys said to me? *'You let a girl break your arm!'* "

Finesse snorted back her tears. She had a caved-in look on her face. "It's not the same thing! That was an accident! You have purposely embarrassed me in front of all those people. I can never go back there!"

Miss Mattie poked her head out of her store. "You two all right over there?"

"Yes'm!" said House. Finesse waved her Snowberger's handkerchief.

"You did it on purpose," said Finesse.

House watched his shadow slide over the sidewalk. "I didn't mean the half of it."

"Yes, you did." Finesse sniffed. "So did the girls at the Lanyard School." She blew her nose.

A bee hummed between them and buzzed off, looking for a flower. House tried to think of something to say. All that would come out was, "We need you."

Finesse blinked through her tears.

"Look," said House. "The Mamas will skin us alive if we don't have a pageant. And the team . . . well, we have to play our game, that's all there is to it, we just do. And you yourself said that we're meant to honor baseball. You said Dr. Dan loves baseball. So did Mr. Norwood. You could direct the play right there on the ball field—there will be plenty of other times to use the stage. We could play some and...dance some. I can't do the play stuff. You need to do it." He took off his hat and scratched his head. "And somebody needs to teach Honey how to tap-dance."

Finesse sniffed. She wiped her eyes with her Snowberger's handkerchief.

"I'm sorry about what I said," said House. "I'm real sorry about it."

Finesse took a deep breath. She looked House in the eye. "I'm sorry about your arm."

His impulse was to say "That's okay," because that's what you said at a time like this. It wasn't okay. But it was what it was. He thought about Pip's words. "I know you are."

"You could be a good actor," said Finesse.

"I'm a pitcher," said House.

"I know you are." Finesse fidgeted. "I tried to say I was sorry last year. I brought you a box of baseball cards..."

"It was *you*?"

Finesse nodded and dabbed at her eyes. "I knew you wouldn't talk to me, so I just left them on the porch. Poppy said you'd appreciate the gesture, that it would give you some comfort."

House nodded. He'd met Sandy Koufax through Finesse—unbelievable. "I don't hate you," he said.

"I don't hate you, either." Finesse swiped at imaginary dust on her black dress.

"So will you do it?" asked House.

Melba coughed politely. Finesse took notice of her for the first time. Without a word she took her veil and hat with feathers from Melba. As she affixed them to her head, she said, without too much conviction, "My uncle, who is paying for our stage and our production, is expecting a play on his stage! Mixing a brutish sport with a fine art is just not done! It's not professional! Aurora County citizens will not stand for it!" But she was intrigued, House could tell.

"It's a compromise," said House. "We each get some of what we want. Everyone who wants to play can play. Everyone who wants to dance can dance. *Everybody gets a part!* It's organic . . . Finesse."

He almost got a smile out of her. "It's . . . imaginative," she had to agree. "Creative . . . in the spirit of the American theater . . ."

"Will you do it?"

And then came another voice, a new one:

"It will never work!" It was a deep, sonorous, basso profundo. Melba, Finesse, and House whirled to face it.

"Uncle Jim-Bob!" cried Finesse.

Dr. Dan Deavers filled the doorway of the barbershop with his legendary presence.

I don't see why you reporters keep confusing Brooks (Robinson) and me. Can't you see that we wear different numbers?

—FRANK ROBINSON, OUTFIELDER, BALTIMORE ORIOLES

"Ohmygolly, Uncle Jim-Bob, what are you doing here so soon?" Finesse fell into Dr. Dan Deavers's enormous embrace.

"Your stage doesn't fit the schoolhouse!" boomed Dr. Dan. "I've come to supervise and to partake of a much-needed vacation!" He took Finesse by the shoulders, lifted her off her feet, and kissed her right in the middle of her forehead. "I see your pageant is morphing into a very interesting amalgamation!"

Finesse began a real boohoo that could be heard all up and down Main Street. Dr. Dan ushered her inside the barbershop and House followed them.

"I'd better get everybody!" said Melba. "Don't say

anything important until I get back!" She ran toward the ball field with her clipboard in her hands. The ballplayers and the rest of the pageant players practically ran over Melba Jane as they raced past her in the opposite direction and flooded into the barbershop. Melba got herself turned back around and joined them.

Pip was not there, but his second-in-command, Mr. Lamar Lackey, stopped his scissors in midclip so he could figure out the commotion. Hampton Hawes was startled awake from where he was snoring in his barber chair, waiting for another customer.

Amid the smells of shaving lotion and the sounds of Finesse's sobs, the whole story was related. Word had gotten round that Dr. Dan Deavers had been spotted at Schotz's Barber Shop, and a crowd began gathering from as far away as Raleigh—even some Redbugs were there with their mamas—all sardined into the barbershop or spilling onto the sidewalk, listening to the saga and sneaking a peek at Dr. Dan.

"It's the best combination of artistic vision and athletic prowess I ever heard!" said Dr. Dan/Jim-Bob, casting an admiring look in House's direction. "I salute you, young House! How did you come up with such a brilliant solution to our dilemma?"

House opened his mouth, shut it, and shrugged. He waited for some kid to tell on him, to tell the whole town that he had been helping Norwood Boyd cook kids, that he was nothing more than a monster himself, but of course no kid would say that in front of a grown-up. No one uttered a peep except for Dr. Dan, who seemed to delight in his own oratory.

"I am a baseball fan of the highest order!" he boomed. "Baseball is an art! A drama! A ballet without music! Let us give it a Greek chorus!"

Everyone in the barbershop smiled good-manners smiles and wondered what the heck that meant. Dr. Dan was happy to explain.

"It's a brilliant solution to combine the game and the pageant, yes, but it will never work unless we go all out! I have learned that when one is presented with an opportunity to become more than oneself, one always takes that opportunity gratefully—one acknowledges all offers of assistance and embraces the larger field, so to speak, of possibility! Let's do it! Let's plan and practice the pageant and the ball game together. We can move part of the stage to the empty lot temporarily as well! It won't fit in the schoolhouse right now, so we'll make good use of it on the field! *Voilà!* A problem turned into a possibility!"

"Voilà!" Finesse beamed. Her uncle was the most handsome, most dashing, most capable man she had ever met. He had coffee-bean skin that glowed right along with his smile and a bushy mustache that was tinged with gray. He smelled like oranges. His enthusiasm was infectious.

"A lot of people are going to think we are a shocking pair!" said Dr. Dan. "But baseball lends itself perfectly to pageantry! This is just what we need—a little drama, a bit of a shake-up in our routines! Is there anyone here from Smith County?"

Several Smith County Mamas raised their hands. "Will you take this proposal back to your ballplayers and make sure we have their complete cooperation?"

They nodded their heads, glancing sideways at one another, their smiles intact.

"Who will step up to the plate to assist us?" asked Dr. Dan.

Inspired, people fell all over themselves in their desire to help.

"I'll mow the ball field and the empty lot!" chimed Old Johnny Mercer, who dug the graves at the Snapfinger Cemetery for the Snowberger's Funeral Home Empire.

"We'll move the stage!" volunteered Woodrow "Pete" Wilson and several of the Papas who were thrilled there was going to be a game.

"I'll starch and press the uniforms!" said Mary Wilson. She stood at the back of the crowd with Leonard Jackson. "My machine's back in business and so am I! *Sunshine Laundry! / Send us your sheets! / Under new management! / We can't be beat!* Where's Cleebo?"

Cleebo had not arrived with the other kids.

"He quit!" cried Ned and Boon.

"We'll just see about that!" said Mary Wilson. "Make way!" She stomped out of the barbershop.

"Where's Honey?" asked Leonard Jackson.

"She went home with Ruby," said Evan Evans.

Mary Wilson pried her way back into the barbershop leading Cleebo by the ear. "Coming through!" she said as she snaked toward Finesse and House. Steam rose from her like she was a pressing machine herself. The look on Cleebo's face was a mixture of pain and fury.

"This boy will play," Mary Wilson stated in a menacing voice. "He will dance, he will sing—" She stopped herself as Dr. Dan stood tall right in front of her. Her eyes traveled up and up until they reached Dr. Dan's eyes. Then her face softened and her voice took on an immediate sweetness. "Have you met my son, Cleebo? Cleebo H. W. Wilson?" She let go of Cleebo's ear, dusted him off, straightened his T-shirt, and shoved him in front of Dr. Dan. Cleebo looked like a mute, deranged dog.

Dr. Dan stuck out his enormous hand and shook Cleebo's smaller one. "Good to meet such an upstanding, cooperative young man!"

Cleebo blinked into Dr. Dan's dark eyes. "Yessir," he mumbled. He cast a sideways look at House, who looked away.

"And you all know my niece Frances!" Dr. Dan hoisted Finesse onto a barber chair—the very same barber chair she'd collided with during her interpretive dance when House's elbow was broken. She balanced herself daintily, standing on the seat of the chair, and gave a small bow.

"Finesse, *s'il vous plaît*!" she sang. "My name is now Finesse!"

"I believe that's the name of a shampoo," whispered Lamar Lackey, still holding his scissors.

"Finesse has more talent in her little finger than I have in my entire body!" Dr. Dan orated.

Miss Mattie appeared at the edge of the crowd. "How much talent does it take to lie in bed in a coma on television for the past month?" But she smiled when she said it. She liked Dr. Dan. She had missed him—everybody had.

Dr. Dan gave Miss Mattie a bear hug. "It takes great talent to figure out how to get out of work long enough for a good vacation, Mattie!" he boomed. "So here I am, coma and all!"

"Well, it's about time," said a voice from the door of the shop. Like the Red Sea parting, a path was opened and through it walked Pip. "James," he said to his grown grandson, Jim-Bob, the famous soap-opera actor Dr. Dan Deavers.

"Poppy," said Dr. Dan, tears in his eyes at the sight of his grandfather. "I'm home."

Regular Edition, June 19

THE AURORA COUNTY NEWS

MURMURS FROM MABEL

By Phoebe "Scoop" Tolbert

As my faithful readers know, I have sworn to deliver the local news just as soon as it breaks, all over Aurora County.

Somehow, even with my reporting skills at their prime, I was scooped! The death of Mr. Norwood Rhinehart Beauregard Boyd was reported in this paper by Comfort Snowberger of Snowberger's Funeral Home. One can perhaps forgive the funeral home for wanting to be the first to report this major event, but I would just like to point out that the protocols and etiquettes of the newspaper business call for fair reportage to all sources as soon as a story is leaked. Please put me back in the loop, Snowberger's.

On to Mr. Norwood Boyd, who, as readers now know, died this past week at the ripe old age of 88. (Not that old; Mr. Tolbert is approaching that age himself! He remembers going to school with Norwood, but of course I don't, as I am MUCH younger than Mr. Tolbert.)

Norwood had a long and industrious career in the U.S. Merchant Marines. He started his life in Mabel, at a time when there were no telephones or toilets in every home. He was known—even as a child—for being a principled person, a man who stood for what he believed in, sometimes at great cost to himself. He was a shining example to us all.

One thing Norwood believed in was people. He brought people together, even after his illness forced him indoors when he could no longer be active. His correspondence was the stuff of legend—Dot Land has had to order an extra mail crate to hold all the mail that has arrived for Norwood just since his death. He was in touch with people from all walks of life, from all his travels, and he championed the human spirit.

Now, there are those who would say Norwood was a recluse. He was. There were rumors of a long-lost love. Who knows. What is true is that Norwood Boyd gave himself permission to stay home for the rest of his life. That was his right.

He leaves behind no immediate family, although he is survived by dear friend Parting Schotz and his granddaughter, Gladys Knight Schotz, and her daughter, Frances Ballard Schotz. He was preceded in death by dear friend Joseph Jefferson Jackson of Greenville, South Carolina, and Joe's great-great-niece, Elizabeth Jackson (maiden and married name) of Mabel, who was also Norwood's goddaughter.

As was reported by Snowberger's, there will be no funeral. However, in related news, rumor has it that the Aurora County All-Stars will play on July 4! Those of you old enough to remember Norwood as a boy will understand that there could be no more appropriate memorial to Norwood Boyd than a baseball game. Play ball!

★ 27 ★

Do I contradict myself?
Very well then I contradict myself,
I am large, I contain multitudes.
—Walt Whitman

"Okay, you got us here—now what?" Cleebo was agitated, and so was the rest of the team. But no one was more agitated than House, who had suggested the symphony true—what had he been thinking?

He had fourteen days to pull together some sort of strategy for beating the Redbugs that would include girls in dresses made of crepe paper toting magic wands made from rolls of wrapping paper. There was not enough time to order uniforms and have them delivered, but there would be matching T-shirts, starched and ironed by the Sunshine Laundry.

"What's your brilliant plan, House?" Cleebo postured.

"Your mama got you here, not me," said House. "And you're not playing."

"What are you talking about?" demanded Cleebo.

"You quit, remember? Go help Frances. That's where your mama wants you, anyway."

"I'm playing ball and you can't stop me—remember what you said when you ruined it for the whole team? Anybody can play! Well, I'm anybody."

"You're nobody," said House. "Wilkie! Gather 'em up!"

Finesse was at the far end of right field, near the Methodist cemetery, surrounded by children who were singing "Aurora of Thee I Sing," a composition Finesse had made up that morning. They sounded like dying monkeys. Melba was waving her clipboard and trying to direct the singing while Finesse tried out a new interpretive dance.

"What are we gonna do with these kids?" asked Wilkie.

"I can throw!" said the shortest kid. His name was Billy. "See?" He picked up a rock, threw it overhand, and hit Cleebo in the shin.

"Hey!" Cleebo took off running after Billy, who screamed away toward town, his short legs pumping up and down like little pistons.

The Tolbert twins, Ned and Boon, trudged into the outfield with girls following them. "Start off playing catch with 'em," said House.

"They don't have gloves!" yelled Ned.

"I can hit!" said little Jimmy Scott at home plate. He grabbed the wooden bat and gave it a walloping once around. He hit the backstop with it and nearly knocked himself out.

"You okay?" called House from the pitcher's mound. So far he hadn't thrown one pitch.

"The bat's cracked!" called Evan Evans from home plate.

And that was the good part of practice.

"Forget this!" yelled Wilkie. "Lot a good it did for you to come up with this harebrained idea, House! We're never gonna be able to even *play* baseball, much less lick them Redbugs! We might as well hang it up!" Wilkie trotted to the edge of center field and stood there with his arms crossed, like a little angry island unto himself. Tutus littered the far reaches of center field.

House wrestled with his doubts. He had insisted they do it this way, but now it made no sense; the boys were right. He'd understood it so clearly the day before. He'd seen it, he'd seen the connections, he'd seen the symphony true, but now, now that he had gotten what he'd asked for, that symphony eluded him. *Listen for the symphony true, House.* He'd laid across the bed the night before with *Leaves of Grass.* He'd inspected it—had Cleebo hurt it? No. Good. He hated that Cleebo had touched this treasure that had belonged to his mother. He hated that Cleebo would make fun of it, of him, of Mr. Norwood Boyd. He hated Cleebo, period.

Thanks to Cleebo, the other kids were looking at him funny. They didn't say anything—they didn't dare, yet—but he could tell they were wondering. Today's newspaper carried Phoebe Tolbert's article. House had read it—every kid in Aurora County had heard about it by now, but no one said a word to him: House's mother was Norwood Boyd's goddaughter, and he, House, hadn't even known it! Questions, he had questions, now, and they buzzed in his mind like a nest full of angry hornets.

Cleebo came back kicking at the dirt as he approached the field. Billy didn't come back with him.

"I'm catching," spit Cleebo. "You can't stop me."

"Watch me," said House.

"I will!" said Cleebo. He stood by home plate, arms crossed, fuming.

"House!" Honey came with Ruby across the field. She carried a small basket of eggs wrapped in a tea towel. She hugged her brother. "I spent the night with Ruby!"

"I know," said House, patting his sister twice on the head. "Honey, we're practicing here . . ."

Chicken feathers decorated Eudora's tutu. She plopped herself down on top of home plate and across one of Cleebo's shoes.

Cleebo's frustration leaked out like a water bucket with holes in it. He marched toward the pitcher's mound. "You said you'd figure this out!" he shouted. He waved his arms up and down. "Look what you done!"

The field was crowded with kids now. House threw a beanball at Cleebo and Cleebo ducked just in time. "Hey!"

Morale was low, but no one was lower than House. He had already missed last year's game. Now he would miss this year's, too, because this game wouldn't be a game.

Honey led Eudora to the third-base line, where she squatted and showed her the eggs in the basket. "Your new brothers and sisters!" she whispered. Eudora wagged her tail and sniffed at the basket.

Three ballerinas came to the plate. "We were sent here by Finesse for our batting practice!" they sang. Sandy Koufax never had to pitch to ten-year-old girls in tutus and glitter shoes. "You're supposed to send three ballplayers to Finesse!"

"What do we do now?" asked Boon. Cleebo parked himself on the All-Stars bench.

"We play," said Ruby. She had two gloves slung over her bat, and her own ball bulging out of her front overalls pocket. She wore her catcher kneepads. She wriggled her catcher's mitt off her bat, pulled the baseball from her pocket, threw it to House smartly, and crouched at home plate.

"C'mon, House," she said. "Let's see that fastball."

"Step out of the box," House directed the ballerinas, who obeyed.

House did a full, high-kicking Koufax windup followed by a long forward stretch toward the plate. He got good underspin on his fastball and zipped it across the plate.

"Strike!" called Ruby. "Again."

House wound up to throw again. And again. It was all clangor, this mess he was in. He'd lost whatever thread he thought he'd found. The more he thought about it, the angrier he became, and the harder he threw. His cap popped off. He threw harder.

"Watch out!" shouted Ruby. "You're going to throw your arm out!"

House threw a blazing fastball. And another. Kids gathered to watch. Finesse came with them.

Over and over House threw in a kind of frenetic ballet of one fluid motion from windup to delivery. Ruby hunkered down and caught every pitch that burned into her mitt—she was that good.

"Slow it down," she murmured. But House wasn't listening to anything but his disappointment. He didn't listen to his elbow, either, as it began to burn a warning. Faster and harder he pitched. Kids murmured in awe and appreciation, but Cleebo knew better.

"Step away!" he shouted to Ruby.

House threw another fastball. Something in his elbow twanged like a tight guitar string. Ruby held on to the pitch instead of throwing it back. House plucked a ball from the bucket by the mound and wound up for another pitch.

"Stop!" Cleebo yelled. He rushed the mound.

House threw a wild pitch. It slammed against the backstop and jingled the chain link like it was broken glass. At the instant he threw, something in House's arm gave out with a rip. House grimaced in pain as he fell to one knee. He cradled his left elbow in his gloved right hand.

Cleebo reached the mound and grabbed his friend.

"Back off, Cleebo!" House shoved him away with his good arm. His left arm was on fire. A sob choked him.

"Oh no!" cried the pageant kids.

"House!" shouted the ballplayers.

"Oh, *mon Dieu*!" whispered Finesse.

"All of you!" shouted House. "Back off!"

★ 28 ★

Any time you have an opportunity
to make a difference in this world and you don't,
then you are wasting your time on earth.
—ROBERTO CLEMENTE, RIGHT FIELDER, PITTSBURGH PIRATES

Honey, House, Leonard Jackson, and Eudora waited in Doc MacRee's office for the verdict. House knew what he would do, regardless of what was wrong with his arm.

"The X-rays show nothing broken, House," said Doc MacRee, "but you've sprained a ligament in your elbow. You'll heal. And you'll play again. But you need to rest it for a week or two. That game is going to be a problem..."

"The game's no problem," said House, tears of relief slipping down his cheeks, disappointment rising like bile in his throat. "I quit."

"What?" House's father let Honey slide off his lap.

"I quit!" said House. He couldn't help crying now and

he didn't care. He felt like something broken, sitting there with a rag of an arm and a worn-out heart. Honey tiptoed over to her brother and massaged the roundness of his knee like it was a mound of cookie dough and she was patting it into shape.

"It would be best to rest it, Leonard," said Doc MacRee. Leonard Jackson nodded.

They sat in silence on the ride home, as if they were carrying a corpse in the back of the truck. Honey's eggs went under a heat lamp in the shed. She was wilted over like a little flower and flushed in sleep. House refused supper and sat on the front porch with a bag of frozen peas wrapped in a dish towel on his elbow.

As soon as his father had put Honey to bed, House peppered him with questions. "Why didn't you tell me about Mama being related to Mr. Norwood Boyd?"

"She wasn't related, exactly," said his father. "But I know what you mean."

"Why didn't you tell me?"

"I don't know, House. It didn't . . . come up."

"Why didn't you bring it up?"

"I suppose I could have. I didn't know Norwood. Your mother did. After she died, I was busy with you and Honey . . . and my own sadness. And yours."

House adjusted his peas, removed his baseball cap, and tossed it onto the porch planks.

"I should have known about it," he said. "Somebody should have told me."

"You're probably right," said his father. "You're a quiet boy. I didn't think to tell you." His father sat down. "I don't always do it right, House." His voice sounded as worn-out as old tires. "I guess what I've really got going for me is I work at it. What else do you want to know? I'll tell you whatever I know."

"I want to know everything."

"I'm glad you're asking."

A long cream-colored car crunched up the driveway. Pip sat behind the wheel. The girl sitting next to him had to be Finesse. House buried his face in his hands.

"Not her."

Yes, her. But she looked different. She was dressed in a pair of shorts and a plain black T-shirt. She wore black flip-flops. Her hair, usually a wild and wiry explosion, was plaited into neat rows. Her face was scrubbed clean. She looked like someone else, someone House used to know. Under her arm she carried her straw tote bag.

Pip gave a wave toward the porch as he climbed out of his car. "I came to check on the young squire here, and to see if you were done servicing my 'lectric clippers, Leonard."

"Just finished them up today," said Leonard, lifting a hand in return greeting. "They're in the workshop."

"Let's go visit 'em," said Pip.

Leonard patted House on the shoulder. "I'm ready to talk when you are." He walked to the shed with Pip in the spangled light of early evening.

Finesse leaned against the porch railing. "What did Doc MacRee say?"

"It's a sprain."

"Can you play?"

"No."

"Do we have someone else who can pitch?"

"We need Koufax if we want to win this game. Do you know who that is?"

Finesse shook her head.

"Sandy Koufax. He's the greatest baseball pitcher who ever lived. He's in that box of cards you gave me. Do you want them back?"

"You'll have to ask Uncle Jim-Bob," said Finesse. "They're his."

"Really?" House rubbed at his chin with the back of his hand.

"Really. Poppy told me I could loan them to you." She rummaged in her tote bag and pulled out a green book. "I've got something else to show you. I've got one, too."

House blinked twice, hard, as if to clear his vision. Of course there would be another copy of *Leaves of Grass*—there were probably thousands. Finesse opened the book to the front inside cover and showed it to House. *Gladys Schotz* was written in a careful script, the same script that was on the inside of his book. *From your friend, Elizabeth.*

"We used to play together when we were little, you and I," Finesse said. "Our mamas were friends."

House rocked back in his chair and let out a long breath. "Yeah."

"I remember the symphony song, too."

House rocked forward and stopped cold. "You do?"

Finesse nodded. "My mama sang it."

Little birds were singing in the pecan trees; it was so perfect. House held his breath. And, right there on House's front porch, as the sun began to dip behind the pines and shadows slanted long across the dirt yard, Finesse sang the symphony song in a soft, sweet voice and in no hurry.

House felt every note, right down to the tingling in his toes. He didn't know where to look, so he stared at the empty clothesline. He had no words.

"Are you okay?" asked Finesse when she'd finished.

"Yeah. Just thinking."

"The symphony true," said Finesse. "I think it's what's left when all the noise stops, when you get quiet and listen for your own true heart."

House adjusted his peas. A rosy light lay over the front dirt yard, spilling onto the goldenrod by the woods.

"What are you thinking about?" Finesse asked, as she tucked *Leaves of Grass* into her tote bag.

"I'm thinking about Pee Wee Reese."

"Who's that?"

"He's a shortstop."

"Is he good?"

"Real good."

"What does a shortstop do?"

"He plays between second and third base. He snags most of the ground balls and he covers second base in a double play."

"Does this Pee Wee live near here?"

The corners of House's mouth turned up in a smile. "No."

"Too bad," said Finesse. "We could use a good shortstop, yes?"

"We could," said House, and he looked at Finesse. Her face wore such an earnest look. House reached into his mind and a question suggested itself. "What's the French word for *toad*?"

"Why would you want to know that?"

House shrugged and put his hands on the arms of the rocker. "There's a lot of 'em around here."

Finesse pulled an English-French dictionary out of her straw tote bag. House watched her leaf through the pages. She ran her finger down a page and considered what she found there.

"Crapaud," she said. Then she giggled a real girl giggle.

House smiled so widely his ears ran back along his scalp. *"Crapaud?"*

"Oui!" said Finesse with another giggle. *"Crapaud!"*

House couldn't help himself. *"Crapaud!"* he hooted. And he laughed. The peas fell onto the porch planks.

Finesse laughed, too, as the evening breeze started to push the sun down so it could cool the day. "So I'll see you tomorrow?"

House shook his head. "No."

"Why not? You could coach..."

"I'm done," House said. "I thought I knew something, but I don't."

"Well...I know something," said Finesse. Her voice was shot through with surety.

"What?"

"We need you," she said. "You're part of the symphony true."

It is a beautiful truth that all men contain
something of the artist in them.
—Walt Whitman

House's father waved good-bye as Pip and Finesse disappeared down the lane. "Almost done," he said to House as he walked back to the shed.

House ate some cold supper, showered until there was no more hot water, and went to bed early on the sleeping porch with *Leaves of Grass.* His heart etched itself around every memory of his mother he could muster, every memory of Mr. Norwood Boyd he could imagine.

Soon he sensed a presence in the shadows at his door. "I know that book," said his father.

House's face colored up. "It was Mama's. Mr. Norwood Boyd gave it to me."

His father nodded. "I remember it. Let me show you

my favorite." House handed him the book and his father took it with great tenderness. "Let's see, where is it... It reminds me of what a symphony people make together."

House blinked. "What did you say?"

"Your mother used to say it all the time," said his father. "'No matter what happens,' she'd say, 'it's part of the symphony true.' She even said her death would be part of the symphony."

House swallowed. "Do you believe that?"

His father rifled carefully through the book, looking for his favorite poem. "I guess I do. We take the bad with the good, we take the night with the day... Somehow it all works out..." He smiled at House. "Look, here's the one I like. I'll read it to you."

House lay back against the pillows on the headboard and listened.

I Hear America Singing

I hear America singing, the varied carols I hear,
Those of mechanics, each one singing his as it would be
blithe and strong,
The carpenter singing his as he measures his plank or beam,
The mason singing his as he makes ready for work, or leaves
off work,
The boatman singing what belongs to him in his boat, the
deck-hand singing on the steamboat deck,

The shoemaker singing as he sits on his bench, the hatter singing as he stands,
The wood-cutter's song, the ploughboy's on his way in the morning, or at noon intermission or at sundown,
The delicious singing of the mother, or of the young wife at work, or of the girl sewing or washing,
Each singing what belongs to him or her and to none else,
The day what belongs to the day—at night the party of young fellows, robust, friendly,
Singing with open mouths their strong melodious songs.

House sighed. Their strong, melodious songs. "It's good." He sat up and crossed his legs in the bed.

"Let me see that arm," said his father. "It'll sleep better with a little support." He began to wrap the arm gently in a loose bandage, carefully avoiding the bruised elbow, and House let him. A night breeze raked through the leaves on the trees while the moon hung low on the horizon. Honey snored little-girl snores from her bedroom and Eudora snuffled next to her.

"How are you, son?" asked House's father.

House approached the problem.

"Everything's mixed up."

"Lots of clangor," said his father.

House raised his eyebrows. "Did Mama sing you the symphony song?"

"She did."

"I didn't know that."

"Now you do." His father finished the bandaging and began to massage House's shoulder. "That feel okay?"

House nodded. "The ball game's a mess."

"I know," said his father.

House chewed on his lower lip. "I don't know what to do about that."

"Maybe you don't have to do anything."

"It's complicated," said House.

"I guess it is, son. But at heart, it's real simple. It is what it is. It just . . . is."

"Even if I can't ever play baseball again?"

"Even if you can't ever play baseball again. But you'll play again."

The old clock ticked away time in the hallway. A long time ago Mr. Norwood Boyd had refused to play ball ever again—Pip should have been his teammate. Not so long ago, Jackie Robinson claimed a place on the field for Pip. For Cleebo. Not so long ago, Pee Wee claimed a place for House, so House could stand tall, reach back, and claim a place for Mr. Norwood. In turn, without even understanding what he was doing, House had made a place for Ruby. For Finesse. For the Aurora County All-Stars. And now, in his anger and frustration, he had lost his own place. He had hurt himself.

"I don't know what to do now."

"You can show up."

House sighed, washed in sadness.

"Lie down," said his father.

And like he did when he was a little boy, House slid himself down the headboard and onto the bed. His father covered him with just the top sheet—it was too hot for blankets, although by morning he'd want one. House sank his head into his pillow. He might look like Mr. Norwood Boyd, lying there. Maybe in a hundred years.

"What would Mr. Norwood say if he were here?" asked his father.

House thought about it. "He'd ask me to finish *Treasure Island.*"

Leonard Jackson nodded. "So . . . he'd ask you to finish what you started."

"Yeah," House whispered. He closed his eyes against the day. "Do you think we have any chance of winning?"

His father tucked his son's arm at his side and stroked his forehead once. "You've already won, House."

"Not like that," House said. "I want to win for *real.*"

His father put *Leaves of Grass* on the night table and clicked off the light. In the tenderness that darkness brought, he added one more thought: "House, we are born, we live, and we die. Along the way we learn to love, if we're lucky. That's what your mother taught me."

The night noises faded as sleep came, and House felt it again, that feeling he'd had when he'd thought to combine the ball game and the pageant. It *was* a symphony true, and he was part of it. That's what his mother and Mr. Norwood Boyd had known—they were, all of them, part of the same song. Everything in the world, everything outside the world, all of it. The snakes that slithered in the grass, the crows that called from the trees, the people who lived and died, the stars that hung in the sky. House imagined the life that had been Mr. Norwood Boyd's, the boy. He imagined the life that had been Walt Whitman's, the poet. He imagined the life that belonged to Finesse—the artist; Pip—the barber; Ruby—the catcher; Melba—the assistant; Cleebo—the angry friend; Bunch—the undertaker; and himself, House—the what? What was he? He was many things, just as everyone—*tout le monde*—was many things.

He was his mother's son, for one thing. He had been an old man's friend, for another. He was glad.

Please do not remove these instructions from the telephone pole by the backstop.

To all players on the Aurora County All-Stars July 4th Pageant Team:

How to Hit the Ball

by House Jackson

It is not necessary to spit, beat the plate with your bat, chew gum, or wear a baseball cap. It is necessary to master the fundamentals of batting:

1. Remove all tiaras. Wear a batting helmet, even if it messes up your hair. Your brains are more important than your hair.
2. Pick a bat that isn't too heavy for you. If you fall over when you pick up your bat, it is too heavy.
3. Don't grip the bat at the very end. This is why you look like you are golfing. Don't grip the bat too

close to the sweet spot or the ball will smash your hands.

4. Keep your feet apart, but not too far apart. Save the splits for the pageant numbers. Bend your knees a little but none of that yoga stuff at the plate. And no standing on your toes, ballerinas. This is a ball game.
5. Crouch over a little bit but don't crowd the plate or the catcher can't see. Don't jump backward every time a pitch is thrown. You can't hit the ball while you are jumping backward.
6. Don't close your eyes and swing as each pitch is thrown. You can't hit the ball if you close your eyes. The ball is more likely to hit you.
7. Don't slug your guts out with each swing. Just meet the ball with your bat. That's all you need to do. The pitcher's job is to throw the ball over the plate. If he doesn't (if he throws wide, too high or too low), don't swing at it.

8. If you hit the ball, run. Run to first base, not to third. Don't try to watch the ball while you run. It's your job to get to first base. First base is straight up and to the right of home plate.
9. Take advice. Don't stomp your foot and walk off when you don't get your way. Also, dogs are not allowed to run with people down the baselines. This is an accident waiting to happen.
10. Stay off the field when you are not at bat. And no more fainting. Wear a hat, drink water, bring a fan. It gets hot out here.

Presented as a Primer for Participants
in the Aurora County Birthday Pageant:

How To Dance La Danse Moderne
Or
"You can never have too much glitter."

By Finesse Schotz, Artistic Director of the Pageant,
Student of La Danse Moderne at the Prestigious
Lanyard School in Jackson, Mississippi, and Passionate Devotee
of Dance Greats Martha Graham ("Dance is just discovery,
discovery, discovery!"), and The Amazing Katherine Dunham
("Go within every day and find the inner strength so that
the world will not blow your candle out.")

Dear Pageant Participants:

"The body is a sacred garment." Martha said that. It is so true! And in la danse moderne, YOU are the instrument you play. There are no "right moves" except for the movement that moves you—what do you feeeeel? That is so important—im-por-tant!

We will engage in ear-wiggling, neck-twisting, shoulder-shaking, elbow-jutting, knee-jerking, foot-stomping, and more, in an effort to loosen up the stodgy mental thinking that traps our body's sense of freedom and lightness and inhibits us.

Plan to learn the dances as they are created, step by stretch by twist by wiggle. Wear loose-fitting clothing to each practice.

Practice dancing barefoot. Be prepared to wear appropriate costuming, which will include bark, ribbons, fur (fake, of course), beads, tights, colanders, face paint, leaves and twigs, and whatever else appears.

Have fun! La danse moderne is nothing if not an interpretation of your spirit's sweetness and pain, as well as an expression of the joy of life and living!

Gehrig had one advantage over me.
He was a better ballplayer.
—GIL HODGES, FIRST BASE, BROOKLYN DODGERS

The next week brought a flurry of activity to Halleluia. The stage was set up near the first-base line on the ball field. The Methodist church became the greenroom where dancers, singers, and actors could change costumes during baseball innings. The Sunday school rooms buzzed with excitement and sparkled with glitter. Mamas sewed their fingers off. To satisfy their mamas and get it over with, every single ballplayer grudgingly agreed to perform one dance together at the end of the ball game. Tights were special ordered for this special number. Flowered tights. Mary Wilson did the fittings herself. Finesse tweaked her choreography and honed her directorial skills. And House—House had his hands full.

No one mentioned Cleebo's accusations about Norwood Boyd. No one mentioned House's speech about Norwood Boyd. But kids seemed to stay an extra step away from House, and eye him with a morbid curiosity.

Nevertheless, for days he stood behind Ruby like an umpire and held pitching tryouts. Wilkie couldn't see the strike zone. Arnold threw fifty-five-footers. Evan Evans threw lollipops—wide ones. Lincoln Latham wouldn't give up his position at second base. Cleebo was the only All-Star, other than House, who could get enough pitches over the plate to qualify him as a pitcher. And Cleebo was uneven. He had already hit Arnold Hindman and three pageant players.

The day before the pageant it all began to come together. Ruby covered home plate. Cleebo pitched. Boon played both left field and shortstop. They would play with one down, but they would play.

"Throw it in here, Cleebo!" shouted Ruby. She crouched into position at the empty plate and gave Cleebo a signal. Cleebo nodded, wound himself up like a pretzel, and lunged forward with the baseball.

Ruby scooped Cleebo's lowball and lobbed it back to him. "I call for curveballs and you deliver swan dives! I call for fastballs, you give me high and outside! You got to throw the ball over the plate, or we'll be here all day!" She punched her glove with her fist and crouched back into position. She wore brand-new shin and kneepads and a catcher's mask that Cleebo clearly coveted, although he would never admit it.

"You give me a little practice and I'll be the best pitcher you ever saw!" said Cleebo. He glared in House's direction. House ignored him. Cleebo had no interest in pitching.

Cleebo threw a ball so far inside Ruby had to scramble to catch it. She missed. "You would've hit that batter!" she yelled.

"I'm doin' the best I can here!" Cleebo hollered back. "It would help if you'd start catching!"

"Don't heckle your own teammate, Cleebo," ordered House.

"I ain't gonna wear no tights," was all Cleebo had to say to House. He threw another high cheese.

Ruby picked it out of the air and shot it back to him. "Let's have a batter!" she shouted.

The cornerman, Evan Evans, stepped into the batter's box. Ruby signaled Cleebo. Cleebo shook Ruby off. Frustrated, Ruby readied herself for anything. Cleebo pitched a nickel curve and Evan got some pine on it and banged a little daisy cutter out toward second base. Cleebo missed it, but Arnold picked it off easily and tossed the ball to Wilkie, who tagged Evan out at first. Players hooted all around. And Wilkie threw the ball back to Arnold at second, who threw it to Lincoln, who was covering third until Evan could take up his position again.

"Three away!" called House. "Good job!" He flexed his

left elbow. It hurt. He couldn't even clap his approval. "Way to work together!" he said, his voice trailing off to wistfulness.

"We're gonna have trouble tomorrow," said Ruby to House. She caught the ball from Lincoln and threw it to Cleebo. "All these pageant kids are gonna strike out, and every one of those Redbugs are gonna get hits off Cleebo. Either they'll hit off him, or he'll walk 'em. He can't throw a strike."

Finesse and Melba were standing at the ready, beside the first-base line. They applauded along with all the pageant kids, including Honey and Eudora Welty. "Time for the Catfish Clog!" Finesse chirped as Melba ushered the dancers onto the stage by first base.

As a result of Dr. Dan's impassioned speech, the pageant ranks had swelled. Finesse now had almost twenty children to marshal through ten numbers that would be slipped in between baseball innings. For the Catfish Clog, twelve kids in catfish whiskers, fins, and tails trooped onto the stage singing "I'm a Little Fishy" to the tune of "I'm a Little Teapot." When they were done tipping themselves over and pouring themselves out into a cardboard cast-iron skillet with AURORA COUNTY emblazoned on the handle, the other pageant players, including Honey, clapped wildly. The catfish bowed. And Finesse cleared her throat as if she were dying of emphysema. Kids waited for her to speak or pass out.

"I must make a pronouncement, *mes amis*!" she gurgled. She patted on her chest as if she was reminding her heart to beat. "As of a few minutes ago in the greenroom, every pageant player who had volunteered for the baseball game has resigned from the game and will work exclusively on pageant numbers!"

"What?" The words steamrolled over House.

Finesse continued. "I know this will leave the All-Stars with only their original team players to play the actual ball game portion of our pageant—but it cannot be helped!"

House bulldozed to the stage. Finesse continued to address the crowd. "This is in no way a negative reflection on your wonderful *base-ball* game, no! It is rather an enlightened awakening to these thespians' true nature and their newfound devotion to the theater! To *la danse*! To movement and life!"

House took the stage steps in one leap. "What are you doing?"

Finesse leaned sideways and whispered, "They're afraid of being hit by Cleebo's pitching!"

House put on his sunglasses. "I don't believe it," he whispered back. It *was* unbelievable. A rescue. A real rescue.

"What's going on?" yelled Cleebo from home plate.

"It's a renaissance of the ball-playing tradition!" Finesse called out to everyone on the field. To House she whispered, "Go knock yourselves out." Then she called to

Melba, "Bring that clipboard over here, Melba! We've got some rearranging to do!"

"All-Stars!" House jumped off the stage and trotted to the pitcher's mound. "Team meeting!"

The catfish cloggers waddled off to the Methodist church with Melba Jane and the other pageant players. "This is so disorganized!" Melba was fraying around the edges. "Where are my Moon Pies?"

Seven hands shot in the air. "And I'm creamed corn from the garden, too, don't forget," said Mary Ruth Hicks.

Finesse watched them walk off. She stood alone on the stage. She stretched out her long brown arms, raised her face toward the wispy white clouds above her, and whispered, "Carry on! Next inning!"

The team that gathered around the pitcher's mound was the original Aurora County All-Stars plus one new member: Ruby Lavender.

"We got us a real game!" said Boon.

"Don't I know it!" said Ned.

"We're gonna beat them Redbugs!" shouted Lincoln, Wilkie, Evan, and Arnold.

"Beat 'em bad!" they all shouted out of habit, even though they all knew better. Without a pitcher, they were doomed.

House stared into the faces of his teammates as reality hit him in the gut. Here it was, the game he had waited for all year, and now he couldn't play in it. Cleebo stared back at House, then looked at Ruby and Wilkie. He straightened his shoulders and stood tall.

"I'm playing where I don't belong," he said. "We can't beat those Redbugs with me pitching. I'm a catcher."

Ruby looked at House, who looked at Cleebo, who looked at the rest of the team.

"We need a pitcher," said Cleebo. "And I'm not it. House here—he's our man."

"His arm's gone," said Wilkie in a voice that sounded like a soap-opera doctor delivering bad news.

"No, it ain't," said Cleebo. "No, it ain't."

"Stop it, Cleebo," said House. But the words were sweet. And House knew where Cleebo was going with them.

"What are you talking about?" asked Ned.

"I'm talking about Sandy Koufax," said Cleebo. "Koufax pitched when his whole arm was black with bubonic plague."

"Gangrene," said House. "And it was his finger. His elbow was black with . . . something else."

"See? What did I tell you? Koufax never gave up. And all he had was a little camphor oil and an old Ace bandage and some aspirin to help him along."

"He had more than that," said House.

"But not much," said Cleebo, "not much. You're always

talking about how Koufax did it, House, about how great he was, and how he pitched through the pain."

"He ruined his arm," said House. "He stopped playing when he was thirty!"

"You're twelve!" said Cleebo. "And we got a game to win tomorrow. You in or out?"

House hesitated.

"Come on, House," said Ned.

"We can't win without you, House," said Boon.

Ruby took off her mitt, tucked it under her arm, and watched.

"Think you can do it, House?" asked Arnold with such hope in his voice that House approached another problem.

"I can't play with you guys lookin' at me like—"

"Get off it, House," interrupted Cleebo. "We don't care if you read to dead guys. You can read to all the dead guys you want, as soon as the game is over."

"Yeah!" said Evan Evans.

"You're sick, Cleebo," said House.

"I am," Cleebo said, "I admit it. I'll admit somethin' else, too, if you want me to."

Not a soul spoke.

The image of Cleebo crying like a baby inside Mr. Norwood Boyd's house melted into the image of Pip in Mr. Norwood Boyd's uniform, and House shook his head.

"No." He had waited so long for this day. To play a real game of baseball! He wanted it. He spoke to them all: seven boys, one girl, and himself.

"Ruby earned her place as catcher. Agree?"

Cleebo grimaced. Boys nodded. Ruby's face turned the color of her hair, but she stood tall. "Agree," they all said.

"Cleebo, can you play shortstop?" asked House.

"You know I can. But I'm a better first baseman."

"Wilkie, can you play shortstop?"

"No!" everyone shouted, including Wilkie.

"You're at shortstop, Cleebo," said House. "Boon, can you move back to left field?"

"With pleasure." Boon shoved a piece of gum in his mouth.

"So?" asked Cleebo for all of them.

The Aurora County All-Stars looked at House.

House looked at his team.

He held out his aching arm. "Tape me up."

★ 31 ★

I encompass worlds and volumes of worlds.

—Walt Whitman

The next day dawned a blessedly overcast one, although there was a hint of rain on the horizon. House's father had iced, massaged, and taped House's arm the night before. Doc MacRee had iced, massaged, and taped it three times by 4:00 P.M. when game time arrived. He had also fashioned a protective sleeve for House's left arm, from an inner tube that Leonard Jackson had in his shed. "You wear this whenever you're not pitching," he said.

And now the people came. Picnics were spread all around the edges of the ball field. Umbrellas dotted the picnic area. As if on cue, the sun spilled out from behind a bank of red-rimmed clouds and danced on the tops of the umbrellas. Dr. Dan waded from picnic basket to picnic basket, from Aurora All-Star blanket to Raleigh Redbug blanket, his full plate of good food growing ever higher.

At 4:00 P.M. sharp, Dr. Dan started them off by introducing every ballplayer from both teams and every pageant player as well.

"And now!" he intoned—he didn't need a microphone; his golden voice carried over the entire field. "And now, we will begin with our country's song! Please welcome Aurora County's newest tapping sensation, Honey Jackson!"

Honey clicked purposefully onto the stage wearing a beautiful red pair of tap shoes, size two, and a sparkling red-white-and-blue tutu. She carried a basket. While everyone watched her, she arranged her stuffed-animal audience-children at the back of the stage, leaned down, and whispered to them, "Now. Be on your best behavior! Your chicken sisters are at home, just waiting to be born, but your new doggie sister is here, and she's going to dance with Mama—and you have front row seats!" She turned to face the crowd, and summoned her partner.

"YouDoggie!"

Eudora Welty's red-white-and-blue painted toenails tapped up the stairs and onto the stage. She wore a matching sparkly tutu. The Harmony Coronet Band—all twelve members—stood alongside the stage and played "The Star-Spangled Banner" while Finesse—dressed entirely in sequined red and holding a wireless microphone in her manicured fingers—stood on the pitcher's mound and sang.

"She's good!" said Dot Land, a look of surprise on her face.

"My baby!" said Gladys Schotz, her hands clasped beneath her chin.

Honey tapped her heart out to the national anthem. She leaned her little body forward and waved her arms in big circles. She tapped to the left, she tapped to the right. She tapped to the front, she tapped to the back. She made a ferocious clangor while Eudora sat at perfect attention on the corner of the stage, panting throughout the entire dance. Folks all over the field stood at attention next to their picnics and placed right hands over hearts.

"O'er the laaaaand of the freeeeee!" sang Finesse, her voice breaking just a bit, "and the home... of the... braaaaaaave!"

To thunderous applause, Finesse bowed and Honey bowed and Eudora barked—barked!—for the first time ever. Honey hugged Eudora fiercely and shouted, "Thank you very much!" to her fans, bowed three more times, collected and kissed her audience-children, and exited the stage, a bright tapping star. She rushed into Leonard Jackson's waiting arms.

"I did it, Daddy!"

"You sure did!" said her father. Eudora barked again and Leonard Jackson rubbed her back vigorously. "And so did you, Eudora!"

Finesse radiated happiness from her perch on the

pitcher's mound. *"Mes amis!"* she said in her best French. "I hope—*j'espère!*—you will love our performance as much as we loved preparing it for you!"

Loved might have been too strong a word. Or maybe it was just the right one.

House approached the mound and Finesse winked at him as she passed him on her way to the Methodist church greenroom. House gave her a confused look and swiveled his head to follow her.

Ruby pulled her catcher's mask across her face and got down in her crouch behind an empty home plate. "Dish it over, House!"

House ground his heel into the mound and flexed the fingers of his left hand, in and out, in and out. Not too bad. He took the baseball out of his glove, rolled it around in his fist with one hand, and found the stitches he wanted. Ruby wiggled two fingers, signaled a slow curve, and House nodded his agreement. He adjusted his grip, toed the mound, wound up, and delivered. The muscle stretched—he could hear it sing. He reminded himself that Sandy's elbow was black, his wasn't. He could take it easy. He could get it over the plate. And Ruby could catch it.

"Play ball!" bellowed Dr. Dan. He clicked on his umpire vest. Cheers ran all the way up the flagpole by Halleluia School.

Kids took their positions. The Redbugs were up first. Cleebo swaggered at shortstop. "Just call me Pee Wee!" Wilkie caught well at first base. Melba Jane started off as the first-base foul judge. She held an open parasol with both hands, using it as a shield whenever the ball was hit. Finesse, who had been memorizing baseball lingo as if it were a script, was a star. She reported the play-by-play, barking into her real, working microphone. She wore a red baseball cap during each inning's play. She liked her role so much, she pulled Melba off the first-base line after the first inning and put her in charge of the pageant.

"The pageant is practically running itself now!" she said. "The order of events is on the clipboard, everyone knows what to do! I have been called to another shore, as an explorer, as a teammate, and you are being summoned to fill the great one's shoes."

"The great one?"

"Moi!" said Finesse.

Melba, happy to be away from the ball game, wrinkled her nose at the pages on the clipboard, pages filled with doodles and lines and arrows, and tried to make sense of it all.

In the greenroom, Lurleen pressed, Mary Wilson pinned, and Mamas helped pageant players dress, then dashed back to their picnics to watch the spectacle. The game emanated from within. It was organic, a renaissance of the ball-playing tradition. Between innings the play flourished. House's father, along with hometown friends, shouted encouragement from the sidelines. A gaggle of girls wearing crepe paper dresses danced the glories of Aurora County, from her pine forests to her white clapboard churches, to her sandy dirt roads and old, kaput sawmill. The Harmony Coronet Band marched across the outfield and played "Waltzing Matilda." Old Johnny Mercer jumped up in a moment of fervor to play the spoons, which led several couples to spontaneously square-dance.

Buoyed by the crowd and the attention, the All-Stars played better than they'd ever played. House took them to a 6–1 lead. He took his time. He prayed for his arm to hold out. He straightened it and stretched it after every pitch, in just the way that Doc MacRee had showed him. Between innings, he plunged it into a cooler of ice water that sat on the end of the All-Stars bench. Then Doc MacRee wrapped it and massaged it.

At the bottom of the sixth, Doc MacRee looked worried. "You need a pinch hitter," he said. "This arm isn't good." House had struck out every time he'd come to the plate.

"We don't have one," said House. As he pitched the next inning, House's shoulder throbbed; his elbow screamed. His curve was gone. He threw nothing but fastballs, no matter what Ruby signaled, but they didn't look like fastballs anymore.

"S'okay, House, just pitch 'em over," called Ruby. And

that's what he did. He got them over. And the Redbugs hit them.

With two outs in the top of the seventh, Jimmy McBrayer slugged a line drive past Cleebo. "Gaaaaa!" Cleebo reached for it and kissed the ground instead. Ned scooped it up, sent it flying to Lincoln at second base, but Lincoln couldn't get it to Wilkie before Jimmy raced across the first-base bag. House rolled his shoulder and talked to his arm.

"Come on, pitcher, come on, pitcher!" yelled the All-Star fans.

"Come on, House!" Finesse yelled into the microphone.

T. P. Edwards knocked a double into left field. Boon raced after it and threw it hard to Evan at third, but Jimmy McBrayer was already there.

"A double into left field!" screamed Finesse. "The play's at home now!"

Evan shot the ball back to House. "We know that!" he shouted to Finesse.

House's arm wailed at him to stop, but he wouldn't hear it.

"Easy does it!" called Ruby.

House wound up and threw again, but his pitches were wobbling and Rex Brown got to first base on balls.

Redbug fans were wild—the bases were loaded. The All-Stars chattered like crows in a field. "Hang in, House! Attaboy, House! One more out, one more out!"

But the next five Redbugs each got a hit off House, and the Redbugs brought in a runner on each hit before Jimmy Swan popped out to Evan along the third-base line and the side was retired.

"Thank heavens!" shouted Finesse.

"Seventh inning stretch!" hollered Dr. Dan.

The score was tied, 6–6.

★ 32 ★

I'm beginning to see Brooks Robinson in my sleep.
If I dropped a paper plate, he'd pick it up on
one hop and throw me out at first.

—Sparky Anderson, second base, Philadelphia Phillies

At the bench, the All-Stars drank deeply and doused themselves with water. The rain had held off, but the afternoon had turned steamy.

"Who's up next?" asked Phoebe Tolbert, who had come to the bench with fresh water.

"Evan, House, and Ned," said Boon. "We'll get 'em, Grandma, don't worry."

"House, get your arm back in that ice," said Ruby. "It's giving out. How are you going to bat?"

"It's fine," said House, plunging his arm up to the elbow in the ice water and wincing.

Mary Wilson handed out crispy clean T-shirts. "You

boys are a mess!" she said, a delighted tone in her voice. "Change shirts!" They did.

While pies were cut, ice was replenished, and lemonade was poured, the Harmony Coronet Band played "America the Beautiful." Melba Jane sang. Folks tried hard not to cover their ears. "Feel it, Melba," whispered Finesse, "feeeeel it!"

"And crown thy good with brotherhood!" Melba crooned. She sounded like a sick seal. Finesse buried her face in her hands. The band marshaled bravely on.

"From sea to shining sea!" She was done. The audience erupted in thankful, thunderous applause. Melba's face lit up like a Christmas candle. "Thank you so much!" she gushed. She picked up her clipboard to resume her duties. The bottom of the seventh inning began.

"Let's get 'em!" shouted Lincoln. He handed Evan his bat.

The Redbug pitcher, Little Mikey McBrayer, chewed a wad of gum as big as his baseball. He spit all over the pitcher's mound. Evan got a base hit. The All-Stars screamed and the fans jumped to their feet.

House came to the plate with his elbow throbbing. He let the first pitch go by.

"Ball one!" called Dr. Dan.

"Good eye! Good eye!" screamed the All-Stars. "Let him walk you!"

"Strike!" called Dr. Dan when the next pitch sailed over the plate.

House readjusted his stance and swung the bat across in a practice swing. He thought his arm might pull out of its socket if he really tested it, but he had to bat—he had no choice. He rested the bat on his left shoulder and nodded at Mikey. The pitch came, and House bunted it, a little tap toward the pitcher. But Mikey was ready. He raced for the ball, scooped it into his glove, and in one fluid motion burned it to first—House was out—and the first baseman shot it to second!

"Slide, Evan! Slide!" screamed House from the first-base line.

Evan threw himself forward and landed with a thud on the second-base bag.

"He's out at second!" yelled Dr. Dan.

"Nooooo!" screamed the All-Stars, but he was. Evan was out.

"Double play!" moaned Finesse into the microphone. The sound carried across the ball field. "Two away!"

Evan and House ran off the field together and clapped each other on the back. "Good try, House," said Evan.

"Good try, Evan," said House. He plunged his arm into the ice water.

"Come on, Ned!" yelled the All-Stars. "Come on, Ned!"

Ned stood at home plate with a resolute look on his

face. He bared his teeth at Mikey McBrayer. Mikey chewed his gum and nodded to his catcher, Jerry Brunner. And, one-two-three, Mikey threw Ned out-out-out. Phoebe Tolbert wept into her Snowberger's handkerchief.

"Curses!" shouted Finesse. "No runs, no hits, no errors!"

"One hit!" corrected Dr. Dan. "Top of the eighth! It's a tie! Six to six! Let's get this show on the road!"

House lifted his arm from the water. Doc MacRee dried it quickly, stretched it gently, and said, "You be careful out there." House nodded and trotted to the pitcher's mound. The crowd cheered.

"Come on, All-Stars!" shouted the team and the fans. "Come on, All-Stars!" shouted Honey.

House closed his eyes and reached deep into his gut. He wrenched up whatever courage he could find there, slapped it onto his aching arm, and he pitched. The Redbugs hit every pitch, but the All-Stars were on high alert now—their pitcher was all but done for. A pop fly to Arnold in right field, a line drive to Cleebo at short, and a little at 'em ball to Wilkie at first.

"Three up, three down!" screamed Finesse as the Redbugs retired and the All-Stars came to bat. "It's the bottom of the eighth inning and the All-Stars are on fire! House Jackson pulls it out of his hat and takes us the distance!"

House ran off the field and to the ice water cooler next to the bench. "Let me have a look," said Doc MacRee.

Leonard Jackson looked over Doc MacRee's shoulder. "Not good," said Doc MacRee. "Get it in the water." The cold water numbed the pain in the ligament, but it ripped at House's skin. He grimaced but forced himself to keep his arm in the water. "Come on, All-Stars!" he hollered in a hoarse voice. "Who's up?"

The Redbugs were on high alert right back. They, too, were carried high on the wind of the cheering crowd. Oh, to have fans! And, oh, to play out the game with such high stakes!

Boon Tolbert got some weight behind the bat and whammed a long one into deep center field. Redbugs outfielder John Caskey got under it and waited for it to fall into his glove.

"Disappointment rains!" cried Finesse.

Lincoln Latham went down swinging at strike three. Redbug parents jumped to their feet cheering at such fine pitching. All-Star parents jumped to their feet cheering at such fine swinging.

And then Cleebo strutted to the plate.

I am not what you supposed, but far different.

—Walt Whitman

Cleebo scraped his shoe on home plate like a horse pawing in place. He hit the dust from his feet with his bat. He spit. He swung the bat across the plate three times.

"I'm ready!" he announced to Mikey McBrayer. "Give me your best shot."

"No outs!" tweedled Finesse. "Let's get a hit, pretty please!"

"Can it, Frances, I'm tryin' to concentrate!" growled Cleebo.

Mikey McBrayer gazed over the top of his glove and nodded his head in agreement with his catcher. He narrowed his eyes and reared back on his right leg, lifted his left, pulled back his right arm, and flung a curve at Cleebo that was high and outside.

"Hey, batter-batter-batter, swing!" screamed the Redbug outfield. And Cleebo swung.

"Swing and a miss, strike one!" boomed Dr. Dan, then "swing and a miss, strike two!"

Cleebo stepped out of the batter's box and spit on his hands. He rubbed them together, stepped back in, and nodded to Mikey McBrayer.

"Take it easy, Cleeb!" yelled House. "Just meet the ball!"

Mikey McBrayer and Cleebo eyed each other. Mikey hiked up his pants, chucked the ball into his glove a few times, rolled his shoulders, spit, and he was ready. He checked in with his catcher, nodded, and threw a fastball straight across the plate.

Cleebo clobbered the ball. It went up. And up. And up. And Cleebo ran. And ran. And ran. The crowd was on its feet screaming.

Cleebo slid into first base. "He's out!" yelled Dr. Dan. And when the dust cleared, everyone could see Redbug right fielder Curtis Ragsdale standing on tiptoe at the edge of the Methodist cemetery, his back plastered against Marie Kilgore's tall obelisk of a gravestone, his arm stretched to the heavens, holding Cleebo's ball in the tip of his mitt.

Cleebo leaped to his feet in disbelief. "It was a homer! It was a homer!"

The Redbug fans screamed their delight. Even the All-Star fans had to holler their congratulations—it was a beautiful catch.

"Three outs! That's the inning!" called Dr. Dan, breathless himself with the excitement of it all.

"Top of the ninth!" Finesse sobbed into her microphone. She had lost all sense of decorum.

House groaned. No way was he going to be able to go back out there yet.

"Great hit, Cleebo!" the All-Stars cried as Cleebo ran across the field toward the bench.

"That's my boy!" hollered Pete Wilson as Cleebo passed his family's picnic blanket. Mary Wilson was in the greenroom. Pete stood up and clapped for his son.

Cleebo stopped and stared at his father. Streaks of dust ran in little rivers down his face where his tears carried them.

"You heard me," said his father. "Nobody can take that hit away from you, son."

Cleebo sniffed. He wiped his nose with the back of his hand.

"Now hold your head up," ordered his father. "Go to work."

Redbug fans cheered for Curtis. All-Star fans mobbed Cleebo. House and Finesse exchanged a look that told

Finesse all she needed to know about House's arm. She took matters into her own hands.

"S'il vous plaît!" called Finesse, as if she'd had a sudden inspiration. "I... I... I have forgotten my most *im-por-tant* number! It is coming to me as we speak!" She twirled up the stage steps, plucked the microphone out of its stand, and began to sing "Beautiful Dreamer" a cappella.

"This is completely unscheduled!" said Melba Jane.

The All-Stars understood what Finesse was doing.

"Is it time, Cleebo?" asked Boon.

"It's time!" said Cleebo, easily distracted, completely recovered, and totally changed. He gestured to the All-Stars. "All right! It's time!" And while Doc MacRee iced House's arm, the rest of the ballplayers rushed the stage just as Finesse finished her song.

"But you don't come on until the end of the game!" Finesse said.

"We got us a plan, too," Cleebo said. And to the crowd he shouted, "We got tights!" From their pockets the Aurora County All-Stars pulled their flowered tights. They dangled them from their fingertips like streamers and then pulled them onto their heads and wore them like stocking caps under their baseball caps, which made their eyebrows bunch above their eyes like woolly worms. They laughed themselves silly while the crowd roared its approval and House's elbow rested.

"Let me see it," said Doc MacRee. He wrapped the elbow in a towel and began patting it dry.

"We been rehearsing our own number!" said Cleebo from the stage. He had changed into a pair of crisply pressed blue jeans.

"I give up," said Melba Jane. She tossed her clipboard onto the stage.

"Clee-bo Wil-son!" Mary Wilson crossed her arms from where she stood next to a platter of fried chicken on her picnic blanket. Cleebo crossed his arms and stared defiantly at the Queen Poo-bah of the Mamas.

"Bravo! Bravo!" thundered Dr. Dan from behind home plate. "An innovation in the midst of our conglomeration!"

"Bravo!" called Finesse into her microphone.

Mary Wilson smiled a smile as wide as the Mississippi River as she considered her good fortune; her boy was on stage in a starring role. And his pants looked great.

House exchanged a look with his father and shrugged. "I don't know what they're doing."

"Hit it!" yelled Cleebo. The Harmony Coronet Band struck up their rendition of "Take Me Out to the Ball Game" and the boys sang it at the top of their lungs, swaying back and forth. They held up peanuts. They held up Cracker Jacks.

Then, in a moment of real spontaneity, Cleebo shouted, "This one's for the Mamas!" Following his lead, the boys danced the second verse. Their arms ballooned like ballerinas. They stood on their toes. They twirled. They swung at "three strikes you're out!" And they ran into one another until they had a seven-boy pileup on their hands and so much laughter they couldn't breathe. House shook his head. He might have laughed if his arm didn't feel as if it were coming off at the shoulder, the elbow, the wrist.

"That's my boy!" screamed Mary Wilson. The Mamas were on their feet, hugging one another, peering at Dr. Dan to see if he was taking notes. Doc MacRee laughed so hard he got carried away unwrapping House's arm.

"Ow!"

"Sorry!"

The boys received a rollicking standing ovation. The Redbugs laughed and pointed. Finesse clapped and bowed deeply in the boys' direction. The boys bowed back. The ovation rang in House's ears as he watched Doc MacRee finish with his arm. He winced as the last stretch was finished.

"We're still gonna beat you, Redbugs!" shouted Cleebo.

"You just try!" yelled Redbug catcher Jerry Brunner. And the two teams were back to their benches, collecting their gloves, balls, bats, and resolve.

Leonard Jackson tugged on the brim of House's baseball cap. He handed him his sunglasses. "I know it hurts."

House shook his head. "It's not bad." He shoved on his sunglasses. It was bad. Even with the little time Cleebo had bought them, he wouldn't last the inning. There was no way they could hold the Redbugs to no runs in the ninth.

His arm was done. It was dead as a doornail.

He told no one.

★ 34 ★

A lot of people in the ballpark now
are starting to see the pitches with their hearts.

—Los Angeles Dodgers announcer Vin Scully,
calling Sandy Koufax's 1965 perfect game

House faced the heat of the Redbug order in the top of the ninth inning: Larry, Curly, and Moe Fortin. Triplets. All of them power hitters.

"You okay?" asked Doc MacRee. House nodded and shook out his arm gently. The pain radiated from his shoulder to his fingertips, but it was worst in his elbow. He checked it for color. Not black. Yet.

"I can do it." He tried not to cringe as he flexed his elbow.

"Just a few more pitches," said his father. "Then you rest that arm."

"Yessir," said House. He would be only too glad to rest it.

"Come on, House!" sang Honey. Eudora Welty panted and wagged her tail.

House smiled at his sister from behind his sunglasses, took a deep breath, and trotted out to the mound.

"The pitcher's mound is throbbing with action!" yelled Finesse. House glanced her way and shook his head. He didn't bother with throwing the ball around the bases or warming up with Ruby. He saved every inch of his arm he could.

"I'm ready," he said to the umpire.

"Batter up!" called Dr. Dan.

Larry Fortin stepped into the batter's box and grinned at House. House gritted his teeth, got his signal from Ruby, and delivered the pitch through his pain. "Gaaaah!" he cried.

Larry hit the ball, a blooper into the infield. House scooped it up, but he couldn't fire it off to Wilkie, so Larry made it to first base. "That's all right! That's all right!" yelled the team and the fans. "Hang on, House! Hang on!"

Curly popped a fly to Cleebo. Cleebo caught it like it was a baby falling out of the sky, with a sweep-back of his glove and a bow. All-Star fans cheered wildly. House could hardly remember the pitch. He wanted to cry with the pain. And that's when Moe strode to the plate with the opportunity to put the Redbugs so far ahead they'd be untouchable.

House was dizzy with pain. Ruby signaled slow balls

but House shook her off. He pulled Sandy Koufax to the front of his mind and he didn't let him go. *Look for me in every atom that you see.* He closed his eyes and saw Sandy in his windup, delivery, follow-through. He saw his mother singing the symphony song as she brought in the sheets on a brilliant summer day. He saw Mr. Norwood Boyd in his bed, breathing his last in the first breath of day. He saw these things more clearly than he saw home plate.

Be with me. He sent the message out into the universe. He dug in his heel, reared backward onto his left leg, lifted his right leg high, pulled back his left arm, gave a loud grunt, and let himself pitch full out.

Moe swung.

"Oomph!" said Ruby as she caught the ball.

"It's in there!" screamed Finesse.

"Strike one!" called Dr. Dan.

House would not allow himself to think about his arm. Again he pulled his vision to mind and threw on instinct, before he could think of anything else.

"Strike two!" called Dr. Dan. Fans rose; their voices broke as they cheered. House was ahead in the count: no balls, two strikes. One more strike and the All-Stars were back in the game.

House groaned loudly with the effort of his next pitch. He heaved it out, he let it go. And his arm let go, too. He was done in.

The fans and the ballplayers held their breaths. The

pitch seemed to float in slow motion across the plate as Moe Fortin swung his bat clean and clear through the strike zone, as the pine made contact with the leather and the baseball sailed through the air, over House's head, over Arnold's head in right field, and over the heads of the tombstones in the Methodist cemetery, where it came to rest on the grave of Anton Land.

"It's gone!" Finesse wailed. "A two-run homer!" Redbug fans went wild. The summer sun blazed out from behind the last of the morning's clouds, as if on cue. Curly and Moe rounded the bases like they were on fire. The score was 8–6 Redbugs.

Cleebo threw his glove to the ground with a disgusted shout, then picked it up with a resigned sigh, and trotted to the pitcher's mound. He clapped House on the right shoulder. "I've got it, House."

House couldn't argue. "Thanks." He ran off the field to ballplayers on both teams slapping him on the back. "Good game, House," they said, and "Not a problem, House, we'll get 'em."

Cleebo pitched the next three batters, and even without a shortstop, the All-Stars delivered. Mikey McBrayer hit a ducksnort into the short outfield and got on first, but the next two batters popped out, one to Cleebo and one to Ned in center field. The side was retired, and the All-Stars walked off the field facing an uphill battle to win the game in the bottom of the ninth. The batting order coming up was a tough one for the All-Stars: Wilkie, who couldn't see well enough to get a hit, Arnold Hindman, who had a penchant for popping out, and Ruby Lavender, who was . . . well, a girl.

"Game's over," murmured Cleebo. He trudged to the All-Stars bench.

Come, said the Muse,
Sing me a song no poet yet has chanted,
Sing me the Universal.
—Walt Whitman

House lifted his arm out of the ice. He couldn't help the tears that slid across his cheeks.

"I love you, House," said Honey. She wore her most worried expression on her face.

House tried a smile for his sister. "I'm fine, Honey."

"No more," said Leonard Jackson. He looked as worried as Honey.

"It's the bottom of the ninth," said House. "I bat fifth, if we get that far."

"You're not getting that far," said Doc MacRee. "Not today."

Fans, pageant players, and family members stood at eager attention in the midst of their picnic debris. Dregs of piecrusts and paper cups were strewn underfoot along with discarded catfish, Moon Pies, and garden vegetable costumes and more: It was the stuff of an afternoon's vigil. The All-Stars had one last chance to win. They needed two runs to tie, three runs to win. They needed a miracle.

The cheering started as soon as Little Mikey McBrayer came to the pitcher's mound with a wad of gum that was as big as he was. His cheek stuck out halfway to Alabama. He had played well all day and he was cocky. His team was about to win. He warmed up with his catcher.

More cheering greeted Wilkie as he stepped to the plate, blinking behind his thick glasses, his knees shaking.

"Come on, Wilkie, come on!" shouted the All-Stars. "Two runs and we're tied! Three and we win!" But Wilkie struck out.

"I'm sorry, boys," he sniffed.

"Sometimes these things can't be helped!" intoned Finesse, in a voice that imparted this information as if it were the deepest mystery of life.

Arnold managed to drive the ball to center and get on first base.

"Man on first!" chirped Finesse. "Very nice hit!"

"That's it, Arnie!" shouted Cleebo. "That's it!" He turned to Ruby, who was in the on-deck box. "Get a hit, Ruby," he said. "Just a hit, that's all we need. Evan's next and he's a power hitter—he can hit you in, just get on base." He spoke in earnest as if Ruby didn't know every player's strengths by heart by now.

"I'll do my best," was all she said.

Mikey McBrayer threw her two strikes and Ruby swung too hard at each one.

"O and 2!" droned Finesse in a funereal voice.

Ruby looked over at House on the bench with his elbow back in the ice. He was watching her. "Just meet the ball," he said. "Nice and easy."

She nodded.

"C'mon! Throw her out!" yelled Jerry the catcher. The pitch came across the plate and Ruby swung through and hit it—a little humpbacked liner that hopped past the Redbug first baseman and settled just inside the first-base foul line. Ruby took off for first base.

"Slide!" screamed Cleebo, jumping up on the bench. "Sliiiiiide!"

Ruby slid underneath the throw from right field to first and touched the bag ahead of the ball. Dust swirled like a tornado of chickens fighting at first base. "She's safe!" yelled Dr. Dan.

"Safe!" yelled Mary Wilson. She grabbed her husband and kissed him full on the lips.

"Safe!" yelled Phoebe Tolbert. She grabbed Mr. Tolbert and... didn't kiss him.

When the dust settled, Ruby was standing on the first-base bag, grinning, yelling, "Come on, Evan! Bang it outta the park!"

But Evan struck out. He hit a high fly above himself. He looked up to see if it might scoot behind the backstop. Jerry jockeyed for position, bumping Evan out of the way, and caught the ball against the backstop, then slithered like a snake down the chain link and landed with a thud in the dirt.

Evan hung his head and tried not to cry.

"It's okay, Evan!" Fans clapped and cheered for him at the same time as they cheered for Jerry's catch. Suddenly, as they got down to the wire, it didn't even matter which team they'd come to cheer for; suddenly everything and everyone was worth cheering for and it all mattered terribly.

"Two away!" wailed Finesse. Her voice carried a jagged edge—she was almost hysterical. "Who's up next?"

Every All-Star player, every Redbug player, every fan groaned. Up next was House Jackson.

House pulled his arm out of the ice water and flinched. Fresh tears crowded his eyes. He reached for his glove.

"No, you don't," said his father. "I can't let you do it."

"We can't forfeit now!" cried House. His tears gargled in his throat.

"House, you have done enough," said his father. "You cannot play!"

A hush fell over the bench. The All-Stars stared at House's grief-etched face and felt as if their best friend had just died.

And then. There was rustling and murmuring at the back of the crowd. Dr. Dan cleared his throat. "We have a pinch hitter!" he called out in his golden voice. "A pinch hitter for the Aurora County All-Stars!"

And as the new hitter revealed himself to shouts of recognition and ripples of appreciation, House wiped his eyes and stared. Then slowly, he stood up.

"'Oh, earth, you are too wonderful for anybody to realize you,'" whispered Finesse. "It's positively Thornton Wilder."

The new player stepped up to the plate—he was old and short, with a stubbly spray of silver gray hair across his head, black shiny eyes, and skin the color of the pinecones that dotted the forest floor. He was the only player wearing a uniform. AURORA ANGELS blazed in a beautiful sky-blue script across the white jersey. The uniform fit perfectly.

Folks held their breath. Cleebo nearly choked on his gum.

The past and the present connected. The batter and House exchanged a look. House gave one nod to the batter, *Thank you.* The batter gave one nod back, *You're welcome.*

Parting Schotz swung at the first pitch from little Mikey McBrayer. He swung like he'd been swinging a baseball bat all his life. He smacked the ball so hard the crack of the bat sounded like an exploding firecracker. The crowd shrieked as the ball sailed away.

Finesse forgot her artistic decorum and screamed into the microphone, "It's a high fly into left field! Beyond left field! Oh, doctor! It's all the way to the chinaberry tree! It's going, it's going, it's gone! Parting Schotz has dialed long-distance! Oh, Poppy! A *home run*!"

It was. Around the bases flew Arnold and Ruby, waving their arms, triumphant. At home plate the All-Stars piled on top of one another. But Pip took his time. He ran the bases with the ease of an eighty-eight-year-old long-distance runner. He ran with the shouts of his teammates in his ears. He ran with his heart full of the fire of living. He ran across home plate, where he was mobbed by All-Stars, Redbugs, Dr. Dan, and fans of all ages, colors, and descriptions. And Finesse swooned through it all. "The ducks on the pond have swum to shore! The All-Stars win it, nine to eight! Give that man a contract! This game is over!"

It was. The Aurora County All-Stars had won the game, the pageant was over, and the crowd—Redbugs and All-Stars alike—went wild.

The crowd makes the ballgame.

—Ty Cobb, center fielder, Detroit Tigers

As the crowd celebrated, Miss Mattie walked purposefully to the stage, took the microphone from its stand, and cleared her throat. Every face turned to her.

"Friends," she said in a strong, clear voice that rang out across the ball field. "Thank you for coming today. Thanks to all of you who helped make this day possible, including our dear friend Pip, who I know you will all want to continue to thank publicly, and to our dearly departed friend, Norwood Boyd."

Appreciative murmurs rolled around the crowd. Miss Mattie continued. "Norwood asked for no funeral or memorial service, but I would like to take this opportunity to say a few words about his life. We all knew him in different ways, of course."

The All-Stars sneaked glances at House, who was standing as still as a statue, staring at Miss Mattie. Miss Mattie took her glasses and her notes from her pocket. "I knew Norwood Boyd all my life," she said. She rested her glasses on the end of her nose and read. "I believe he was a visionary. He saw our world as it should be. Through his travels and study, he came to believe that we are all connected, deeply and irrevocably, and that hurting one of us hurts all of us."

She gazed over the top of her glasses. Then she went back to her reading. "Norwood used to say, 'It is hard to see inside someone's heart unless you have an invitation, and, even then, you must agree to come inside.'

"Norwood came home and he did not stay idle. He worked behind the scenes, creating change through a voluminous correspondence throughout the world. And, although most of you don't know it and won't see how, Norwood worked hard to make this very day happen as well. He had his reasons. And we are the beneficiaries of his goodwill."

Miss Mattie looked up with tears in her eyes. "We are his family," she said in an uncharacteristic tender moment. "We are each other's family. This is what Norwood Boyd knew."

She took off her glasses, folded them, shoved them into her pocket along with her notes, smartly patted at her bunned hair, and stepped quickly down the stage steps. Mamas and Papas, friends and neighbors, pulled Snowberger's handkerchiefs out of their picnic baskets and dried their eyes.

House didn't try to stop his tears. They slid slowly down his cheeks as his heart beat strong and steady in his chest.

Pip handed him a Snowberger's handkerchief. "Dry your eyes," he said.

"Yessir," said House. He blew his nose, too.

"I gathered up some things for you," said Pip. "You come see me tomorrow."

"Tomorrow," repeated House.

It was time to go. Ballplayers slapped one another on the back, congratulated each other, made plans for next year. "Good game! Good game! Next year! We'll beat the pants off you next year! Oh yeah? Yeah! Well, come on! We'll be ready! Good game, House! Good game, Mikey! Good game!"

"You playin' tomorrow, Ruby?" Ned called.

"I'll be there!" Ruby called back.

As families packed up their picnics and headed for home in the slanting light of early evening, Cleebo walked away from everyone and sat on the All-Star bench, alone.

"Cleebo?" Mary Wilson had her arms full of costumes to be laundered and starched.

"I'll be along directly," said Cleebo. "Please."

"Take your time," said his father. "Great game, son. Great game."

"Thanks," said Cleebo. He smiled a lopsided smile.

"Let me help you with those, Mary!" said Dr. Dan. He scooped the costumes out of Mary's arms and handed some to Finesse. As the little group made its way to the Sunshine Laundry truck, Finesse curved her fingers in House's direction, a little up-and-down good-bye. House lifted his good hand in reply.

"Au revoir," whispered Finesse.

The dazzle of day was gone. The clangor, the chorus, the perfect band had played out on a spectacular sun-drenched summer afternoon, and now the baseball field was empty. It echoed with the history that had been made there. Now, hanging in the thick summer air was the symphony true, the mingling of every living thing, every heart, every mind, every memory. Katydids sang the evening in as House stood outside his father's truck.

"I'll walk home," he said. His arm was in a sling that Doc MacRee had fashioned on the spot.

"You come into my office tomorrow," Doc MacRee said. "We'll get you fixed up."

"Yessir," House promised. Tomorrow was shaping up to be a busy day.

"See you at the house," said Leonard Jackson, casting a

glance in Cleebo's direction. "I've got applesauce cake left over if you're hungry." Honey slumped over her seat belt in the front seat of the truck, asleep. Eudora snored on the floorboard in front of her.

House walked back to the All-Stars bench to get his glove. Cleebo picked it up and handed it to him. "We beat them Redbugs," he muttered.

"We sure did," said House. He took his glove from Cleebo. His arm throbbed at a low, steady pitch.

"I never saw anything like it," said Cleebo, casting for conversation.

"You never will again," said House.

"How's the arm?"

"I'll live."

"You'll pitch again, too."

"I expect I will."

House slumped down heavily on the opposite end of the bench. He and Cleebo sat there, as still as sleeping flies in the smothering heat. Cleebo's betrayal filled the space between them. The air was alive and hummed with insects.

"I'm a butt," Cleebo said. "You've got a butt for a friend."

House thought about it. "I wonder what the French word is for butt."

Cleebo shook his head. "I don't believe that Frances."

"Me, neither."

"And Ruby!" said Cleebo.

"She's a good ballplayer," said House.

Cleebo had to admit she was. "You got any pie at your house?" he asked. "I didn't get to eat hardly nuthin' all day! All those picnics, and all I got was some deviled eggs!"

House examined the heavens. Cirrus clouds skimmed across the afternoon sky.

"I'd settle for peanut butter and jelly," offered Cleebo. He bobbed from one foot to the other.

House smiled. He popped Cleebo on the shoulder with his glove. "Come on."

And they walked together toward home.

★ EXTRA INNING ★

And your very flesh shall be a great poem.
—WALT WHITMAN

Mr. Norwood Rhinehart Beauregard Boyd, age eighty-eight, philanthropist, philosopher, and maker of mystery, left a will. He wrote it seven years before he died. The witnesses to his signature were Parting Schotz and Elizabeth Jackson. The will called for the formation of a real Little League team in Aurora County called the Aurora County All-Stars. Anyone could play who wanted to play. Anyone. There were to be uniforms, real uniforms, for every player.

Mr. Norwood Boyd's home was to be razed and a baseball field was to be built on Mr. Norwood's property; a baseball field with real dugouts and benches and bleachers for the fans, real bases, a real pitcher's mound, even a snack stand where there would be plenty of cold drinks and hot dogs, plenty of peanuts. There would be plenty of parking as well—there would even be lights. Norwood left money for the construction.

His will held one last bequest. "I bequeath my dog, Eudora Welty, should she still be living at the time of my death, to the Jackson family, from whence she came. As a young pup, Eudora Welty wandered to my house and liked it here, but she was my goddaughter Elizabeth's dog first. Elizabeth allowed Eudora to visit often, and then, finally, she allowed me to adopt Eudora as my companion. It was a loss to young House, who was only two years old at the time. I'd like to return Eudora Welty to House with my thanks. The loan of his dog to me has been a joy in my life. She has been a good friend. Perhaps she will befriend House into his adult years."

She did. When she wasn't befriending Honey.

Pip gave House the seventeen books that House had read to Norwood Boyd. House kept them on a shelf in his room, all but one. He put *Treasure Island* on his night table. He left the ribbon in its place inside the book, where it waited for him, someday—perhaps when he was an old man himself—to open that book to where he had left off and read the rest of the story.

★ ACKNOWLEDGMENTS ★

The characters in this book set up a clangor in my mind and heart a few weeks before I was invited to write a serial story for the *Boston Globe,* which is where this novel's seeds were planted. To prepare for the *Globe* assignment, I researched the conventions of the Victorian serial novel and fell in love with cliff-hanging suspense, magical mystery, oaths of secrecy, moral dilemmas, matters of identity, coldhearted revenge, startling surprise, dollops of sentimentality . . . and dead guys. Wilkie Collins, a master of the serial novel, purportedly said, "Make 'em cry, make 'em laugh, make 'em wait . . . in exactly that order." That's what I tried to do. Thanks to Steph Loer and everyone at the *Globe,* that organ majestic, for giving me the opportunity to stretch and grow as a writer.

I had a chorus of help in writing this novel: Little League ballplayers who understood baseball, friends who championed American civil rights and baseball history, readers who revered Walt Whitman, kids who cherished tutus and the stage, grown-ups who loved dogs. They came out of the woodwork. Terry Berkeley wrote eloquent passages on what it felt like to play baseball as a kid, which reminded me of how much I loved the baseball I knew as a kid, the heroes my brother Mike emulated, the baseball cards he and Larry Joe Stoffel traded every Saturday afternoon, and the sandlot ball we all played in the back lot we had cleared with our families in Camp Springs, Maryland.

I wrote this novel with these choruses in mind. Once I had a complete manuscript, Zach Wiles, philosopher, read it carefully and offered solid, constructive feedback. Jerry Brunner, poet, loaned me his prized volumes of Whitman and directed me to particular passages he loved. My friends and family in Maryland, Mississippi, and Georgia sounded all the right notes of encouragement as I swung and struck out with various deadlines and dinners and family plans. They were so faithful!

Family sustained me through the dark, dark nights that novels inevitably possess. Jim Pearce showed to my eyes the stars. Hannah Wiles remained a faithful and generous

correspondent. Deborah Hopkinson clapped her hand on my shoulder, my compatriot. The Mings gathered round with a cheerful fire, tea, and toast. My students—Jandy, Mary, Teresa, Cheryl, and Jonathan—inquired after me often, turned in their work on time, and forced me to be disciplined about my own process. My colleagues in Vermont—well, thank you.

Then there is my editor, Liz Van Doren, who believed there was a full-fledged novel waiting to grow from tiny seeds. She completely dazzled me with her willingness, generosity, sensibility, tenacity, and eagle eye. I depended on her. She sent me back to the page more times than I can count, always with challenging questions and high expectations.

I'm grateful for the art that existed in the world before I came to write this story. I relied on *Leaves of Grass,* of course, as well as *The Portable Walt Whitman* (edited by Mark Van Doren), and *Sandy Koufax: A Lefty's Legacy* by Jane Leavy. While revising this book I listened to a wonderful CD, *Leaves of Grass,* Whitman's poetry set to music by Fred Hersch, particularly the cuts "After the Dazzle of Day" and "Song of the Universal," sung by Kate McGarry and Kurt Elling. I also kept nearby for comfort a copy of Charles Dickens's *Great Expectations,* a book that was assigned reading in my tenth-grade English class in Charleston, South Carolina. Thank you, Mrs. Ackerman.

This is the third book in the Aurora County trilogy of

novels. "Come," said the muse: How fortunate I am that Ruby Lavender showed up some years ago with her grandmother, Miss Eula, whispering in my ear. Then Marla Frazee came along to give a vision and feel to Aurora County with her transcendent covers. Designer Vaughn Andrews pulled that look together. All three books have been lovingly created and cared for by everyone at Harcourt in New York and San Diego, including Kate Harrison, Gretchen Hirsch, Mary Machado, Robin Cruise, Dan Janeck, Lydia D'moch, Julie Tibbott, Lori Benton, Paul Von Drasek, Jen Haller, and everyone in children's marketing, especially Steve, Barb, Sarah, Kia, Ellen, and Amanda. Thank you all—you are a perfect band.

Finally, thank you to readers everywhere for reading and sharing these stories. Here is what I have learned from you: Those we love never leave us, they are only transformed. They live on in our hearts, silently moving athwart our souls, part of the symphony true.